P9-DVS-287

Five Nights at Freddy's™

FAZBEAR FRIGHTS #10

FRIENDLY FACE

Five Nights at Freddy's™

FAZBEAR FRIGHTS #10

FRIENDLY FACE

BY

SCOTT CAWTHON
ANDREA WAGGENER

Scholastic Inc.

If you purchased this book without a cover, you should be aware that this book is stolen property. It was reported as "unsold and destroyed" to the publisher, and neither the author nor the publisher has received any payment for this "stripped book."

Copyright © 2021 by Scott Cawthon. All rights reserved.

Photo of TV static: © Klikk/Dreamstime

All rights reserved. Published by Scholastic Inc., *Publishers since 1920.* SCHOLASTIC and associated logos are trademarks and/or registered trademarks of Scholastic Inc.

The publisher does not have any control over and does not assume any responsibility for author or third-party websites or their content.

No part of this publication may be reproduced, stored in a retrieval system, or transmitted in any form or by any means, electronic, mechanical, photocopying, recording, or otherwise, without written permission of the publisher. For information regarding permission, write to Scholastic Inc., Attention: Permissions Department, 557 Broadway, New York, NY 10012.

This book is a work of fiction. Names, characters, places, and incidents are either the product of the author's imagination or are used fictitiously, and any resemblance to actual persons, living or dead, business establishments, events, or locales is entirely coincidental.

Library of Congress Cataloging-in-Publication Data available

ISBN 978-1-338-74119-3

1 2021

Printed in the U.S.A. 23

First printing 2021 • Book design by Jeff Shake

TABLE OF CONTENTS

Edward's cereal bowl hit the floor and shattered; milk and soggy flakes splashed his jeans. Edward jumped up, frowned, and looked around, reminding himself of where he was. *Right.* He was in the kitchen—old-fashioned red laminate counters, bright white farm-style sink, retro fridge and stove, smells of ripening bananas and the alfalfa his mom put in her "energy smoothie"—he'd been eating breakfast until he got lost in his book. He looked down and stared at the remains of his bowl.

"Edward, you have to be more careful!" his mom snapped.

Edward glanced at her. His mom looked harried, as usual. A few auburn strands had come loose from the twist she always wore her hair in. She was shaking her head and rubbing her temples as she stared at the mess on the scuffed hardwood floor.

"How'd that get down there?" Edward asked.

His mom sighed. She leaned over and started

picking up pieces of green stoneware. Edward bent over to help her . . . and their heads bumped together.

"Ow!" they shouted in unison.

His mother straightened and scowled at him. In one hand, she held the stoneware shards. She used the other hand to probe the red spot on her forehead.

Edward opened his mouth to apologize, but a look from his mother silenced him. She walked to the trash can under the sink and dropped in the broken cereal bowl. Edward grabbed a napkin from the round kitchen table, squatted, and started wiping up the milk and cereal.

"Edward."

His mom held out a wet rag for him to use on the floor. He took it and started swiping it this way and that. His swift motions flung bits of cereal farther across the floor.

His mom sighed again. "Just leave it. I'll get it. Go brush your teeth. You're going to miss the bus."

Edward stood and seized the moment to apologize. "Sorry. I don't know how that bowl fell."

His mom opened her mouth, closed it, took a deep breath, and then reached out and ruffled his hair. He squirmed. He wished she wouldn't do that. It was like she couldn't tell the difference between *eighth grade* and *eight*. She still tried to treat him like a little kid, even though he'd been thirteen for months. He was a *teenager* now. He needed her to get that.

He looked at her tight face. Now probably wasn't the best time to try to explain it, though.

Edward and his mom had been on their own for a long time, and for the most part, they were close. They looked alike, too, which could be embarrassing. Even with the subtle makeup his mom wore, her hazel eyes, small nose, wide mouth, and strong jaw were almost mirror images of his own features. It was uncanny. His hair was the exact color of hers, too—but his hair wasn't long enough to twist.

"Well, my little science geek," his mom said, "what was that question you were asking the other day about unstoppable forces?"

"What happens when an unstoppable force meets an immovable object? That question?" Edward scrunched up his face. What did the irresistible force paradox have to do with anything?

His mom nodded. "That one. Well, I can't answer it. But I do know what happens when a cereal bowl pushed to the edge of the table meets the elbow of an inattentive boy who is reading at breakfast instead of eating."

"Not a boy," Edward said.

"Fine. Teen. Same result. You need to focus on one thing at a time, Edward. You get in a hurry, and that's why you're so prone to accidents. If you want to live through your teen years, you need to *pay attention*."

"Well, I was *paying attention* to what I was reading," Edward said.

"That's not—" His mom sighed again. "Go pay attention to brushing your teeth."

Edward shrugged and turned to leave the kitchen.

"Your book?" his mother said.

"Oh." He turned and took it from her. She shook her head and smiled at him in the lopsided way she had whenever he messed something up. It was like she was saying, "You're a hopeless case, but I love you anyway."

Edward hesitated, then hugged his mom. "Sorry."

"Edward, are you listening?"

Edward looked up at Mrs. Sterling, who frowned at him from the front of his eighth-grade science class. "Sorry?"

"I asked if you could please grab the iron filings from the cabinet. You're the closest to it."

"Oh. Sure." Edward turned around and opened the metal cabinet behind him. They'd been talking about the whole unstoppable force/immovable object thing again at the start of class today, and his brain couldn't stop chewing on it. Thanks to his many questions about it, Mrs. Sterling had assigned a paper on the subject. He thought about how he was going to organize his essay while he grabbed the filings.

"Okay, so now we're going to witness the power of magnets," Mrs. Sterling announced.

She beamed at the class. Mrs. Sterling was middle-aged with a round face and a wide smile. She always looked like she was having the time of her life, even when she wasn't. She presided like a game show host over the classroom, which was full of desks, lab tables, and cabinets of vials and beakers. Charts, diagrams, and photos of scientific anomalies littered the walls—an endless number of distractions for Edward's curious mind.

"Edward, since you're up here," Mrs. Sterling said, "why don't you sprinkle those filings on that magnet?" She pointed to a flat gray boxlike contraption on her desk before turning away to write something on the blackboard.

He tried to see what she was writing while he opened the vial he'd grabbed, and, without looking, sprinkled a mound of filings on the flat surface.

"Thank you, Edward," Mrs. Sterling said. "You can return to your seat."

Edward nodded and headed back to his desk.

"Okay, here we go." She flipped the switch on a fan that was set up in front of the magnet.

Suddenly, the front of the class was pelted with tiny black particles . . . and everyone started to sneeze.

Mrs. Sterling, being nearest to her desk, sneezed the hardest. She also closed her eyes tightly.

One of the girls in the front row squealed. Another cried out, "My eyes!"

"Turn off the fan!" a boy shouted. Mrs. Sterling, her eyes still shut, groped around for the fan and ended up knocking it over.

Edward sneezed, and his eyes started to burn. What had happened?

"Are you sure those were iron filings you grabbed?" his best friend, Jack, asked, pulling his shirt up over his nose.

Edward wiped at his runny nose. "Sure, I . . ." He cringed and turned to look at the cabinet.

The vial of iron filings was still sitting there. He'd grabbed the pepper Mrs. Sterling had used in their surface tension experiment a couple days before.

"Everyone out!" Mrs. Sterling commanded in a shrill tone. She was staggering around, tears streaming from her eyes. But she was still smiling.

"Klutz face strikes again!" one of the boys shouted as they all ran from the classroom.

"Sorry," Edward said when he joined his classmates in the hallway. "I . . ." He stopped and shrugged. There was no point in trying to explain. So, he just repeated, "Sorry."

"I wonder how many times a day I say, 'Sorry,'" Edward said to Jack as their bus trundled away from school that afternoon.

"Sorry?" Jack tugged on his earbuds and turned his smiling face toward Edward. "I didn't hear you. Could you please repeat what you said?"

"Nothing."

Jack shrugged and put his earbuds back in. His smile stayed in place.

Jack was nearly always smiling—one reason for that was that his lips were naturally upturned. Another was that Jack was just generally happy all the time. Edward had never known anyone as good-natured as Jack. His warm brown eyes already had faint smile crinkles at the corners.

Edward gazed at the golden spiral on Jack's baggy T-shirt for a second and wondered what Jack was listening to (it was always an audiobook, never music). Then he turned and stared out the window.

The junior high school Edward and Jack attended was part of a complex that also included the town's high school. The complex had been built just the year before to replace the old middle school, which had succumbed to a mold problem deemed too expensive to remedy. The new school complex was nice, but due to a zoning issue, it had been built a few miles outside town. Because of this, the first part of the bus ride home went through a relatively wild area. Or at least, Edward thought of it as wild.

The route cut through a thick forest. Tall fir trees pressed up against one another at the edge of the gravel on the roadside. Most of Edward's classmates loved the woods—on Monday morning in homeroom they'd talk about catching crawdads in the creek, floating all day in a deep swimming hole a half mile or so from the school, and playing king of the hill on what the local legends said were old burial mounds. Edward, however, didn't like the forest. It was too dark, too easy to get lost in. It left a chill on the back of his neck, the idea of the trees closing in, dampening the sound so no one could hear you scream.

Edward shifted on the hard bus seat. The padding under the vinyl was worn, and for an uncomfortable moment, he felt swallowed by his thoughts. When he repositioned, he flung out an elbow.

"Ow!" Jack said.

"Sorry." Edward winced. There it was again. He should start counting. Was the endless repetition of *sorry* a mental condition? Like Tourette's or something? Maybe he had a neurological issue and that was why his elbows, and his body in general, were always getting him in trouble.

He shifted again, and this time, he kicked Jack in the ankle. Jack jerked his leg away and studied Edward.

"Sorry," Edward said.

Jack again removed his earbuds. This time, he put them away. "Do you have something weighing on you? You've been weird all day."

"As opposed to other days? Do you think there's any day that I'm not weird?"

Jack quirked his full lips and rubbed his nose. "You

make a valid point." He leaned over and bumped shoulders with Edward. "But it takes weird to know weird."

One of the girls seated in front of Edward and Jack whirled around and gave them a look. "You're *both* weird."

Edward flushed. The girl, Julia, was one of the most popular kids in his year, which meant she was the antithesis of him. Most days, that didn't bother him. He and Jack had decided a long time ago that they existed in their own universe. They might have to hang out in this one, but theirs was separate. They were sort of like the Loch Ness Monster, which Edward was convinced lived in another dimension and occasionally came through a wormhole to visit this one. Why else would the monster be spotted only ten times or so a year?

He looked into Julia's pretty eyes. He wondered if his theory would interest her. He opened his mouth, but before he could speak, she rolled her bright blue irises. "Thanks to you two, we all have to write papers on why it's impossible for an unstoppable force to exist in the same universe as an immovable object!"

Jack's smile widened, and he bounced in his seat. "What's the issue with that? It's quite entertaining to think about. Just imagine if this bus had infinite energy and—"

"Shut up!" Julia turned around.

Edward stared at the way her wavy black hair hung

from the back of her head like a waterfall cascading over rocks on a moonlit night. He glanced at Jack, remembering Jack's laughter when Edward had shared his feelings with him a couple weeks before.

"Have you lost interest in the sci-fi genre and developed one for romantic fiction?" Jack had sputtered between guffaws. "She lives on a different plane of existence, Edward. It's not possible."

For reasons Edward didn't understand, this universe (not the one he and Jack were from) had its basis in a couple of strange equations.

> Equation 1:
> Interest in science - Interest in sports = Weird
> Equation 2: Weird + Small = Outcast

Who decided this stuff? He wasn't sure. It seemed like nerds generally made more money. Nerds created stuff that made the world better. So who invented this popularity calculus? And who distributed the memo about it? It just seemed to be something everyone knew.

"You coming?" Jack asked.

Edward blinked and looked around. Several kids were getting off the bus. Edward looked out the window. This was their stop.

Jack and Edward stood, but something wet and gooey smacked Edward in the cheek. Before he could reach up, the gooey object—chewed gum— bounced onto his chest and stuck to the left eye of his smiley face T-shirt. He tried to flick it off, but it clung. He grabbed it, almost gagging at the grossness of the slick spittle covering the gum. In spite of that human slime, the gum stuck to his fingers.

"Come on," Jack urged. He was already standing in the aisle.

Edward sighed and pulled on the gum. He got most of it off his shirt and had to hold it as they got off the bus. He was tempted to try to wipe it on a seat as he went down the aisle, but that would be wrong. He'd wait until he got out; then he'd wipe it onto a rock or something.

He looked around. No way of knowing who threw the gum. Anyone in this universe might have.

As soon as Edward was off the bus, the driver, Don—a big, semi-retired man with curly gray hair—called out, "Have a good one!"

Edward waved at Don as the bus doors closed with a *thump*. The bus belched exhaust and rumbled away.

Jack carefully centered his stack of books in front of his belly and asked, "What would you like to do this afternoon?"

Edward watched the other kids meander down the street. He stepped away from the curb and reached down to pick up a rock from the flower bed at the edge of Mrs. Phillips's yard. After a glance at her window to be sure she wasn't watching, he used the rock to scrape the gum from his fingers. Then he bent back down to reposition the rock, gum side down, exactly where he'd found it.

As he set the rock in place, he heard a faint sound. Edward froze and listened. *What was that?*

The bus was nearly at the end of the block. When it turned the corner, the noise of the engine grew fainter. And the sound coming from Mrs. Phillips's flower bed got louder.

It seemed to be a cross between a squeak and a chirp. Was it an injured bird? A chipmunk?

Edward dropped to his knees and began looking around under the big rhododendron shrub guarding Mrs. Phillips's seasonal plantings. Because it was January, the flower bed held no flowers at the moment. Instead, it held a collection of winter-clad gnomes, all of which wore handknit sweaters Mrs. Phillips had made herself.

Whatever was making the sound made it again. It was louder now. *Chwee, chwee.*

"What are you doing?" Jack asked.

"Shh. Don't you hear that?"

"Hear what?"

Edward ducked his head under the bush and gently repositioned a gnome wearing a ski cap.

The sound shifted to a pronounced *hissss*, and he yanked his hand back.

"I think there's a snake in there," he said.

"Well, then why are you placing your hand in that vicinity?"

The hissing stopped, and the sound returned. Only this time, it was more of a *mwee* than a *chwee*.

"Hey, I heard that," Jack said. "A snake couldn't make that sound."

Jack leaned over, brushed off a spot on the sidewalk, and positioned his stack of books at the edge of the flower bed. He knelt next to Edward and leaned in to peer past the gnomes.

Together, Edward and Jack moved another gnome. From beyond their hands, something hissed again and then emitted another *mwee*.

Jack held aside a rhododendron branch, and two yellow eyes peered out at them.

"It's a kitten!" Jack exclaimed. His usual smile turned into a huge grin.

The kitten said again, "Mwee."

"Hello, kitty," Jack said in a soothing tone. "It's a pleasure to meet you, little guy. You have no reason to be afraid. We have no intention of hurting you."

Edward leaned over and craned to see past Jack's outstretched hand. It was dark under the bush, and the only part of the kitten that was clear was its eyes.

"Come on, little buddy," Jack coaxed, his voice an octave higher than Edward had ever heard it. "We can assist you."

Jack turned to whisper to Edward, "I don't suppose you have any cat food in your backpack?"

Edward snorted. The kitten hissed.

Jack whispered again, "I don't think Faraday likes you."

"Faraday?" Edward whispered back.

"You know, Michael Faraday, the famous scientist? He founded two laws of electrochemistry?" Jack was still whispering. The kitten had stopped hissing.

"Of course. Him." Edward grinned. Every day, Jack told Edward something he didn't know. Edward was pretty sure he learned more from Jack than he did at school.

A truck engine revved, and Edward turned to frown at it. On the other side of their neighborhood, some developer was putting in a new subdivision. Heavy machinery had been cutting through Edward and Jack's neighborhood for the last week or so. According to Edward's mother, dump trucks would be going back and forth for months.

The truck's roar faded away. Someone yelled out. The kitten opened its mouth and let out another *mwee*.

"I thought kittens *meowed*," Edward said.

"Kittens have a wide variety of vocalizations," Jack replied. "Their communication is as idiosyncratic as that of the average human. Although the homogeneity of our classmates' utterances argues against human singularity."

Edward frowned and opened his mouth to ask Jack to explain what he was talking about, but Jack went on, "I recommend that you retreat for a moment. I believe I am establishing a bond with Faraday. We'll include you as soon as we've solidified our connection."

"Um, sure." Edward dropped from his knees to his butt and scooted backward. Even though it was cold outside, the cement felt warm through his jeans. He glanced up at the bright sun, then closed his eyes and watched spots dance behind his eyelids.

He listened to his friend "establishing a bond." He grinned.

Edward and Jack had been friends since they were babies. Could babies even *be* friends? According to his mother, Jack and Edward played together before they could walk. He wondered what they did. Did they drool on each other?

At any rate, to say that Edward and Jack "grew up" together might be overstating things a bit. Neither one of them had managed to reach anything approaching a normal height for their age. Consequently, they'd been relentlessly teased from the moment they entered school. But honestly, even if Jack wasn't short, he would still invite derision. It was the way he talked. And the way he thought. Take the question about cat food, for example. He wasn't kidding when he asked that. Jack got into physics when he was barely old enough to read. His understanding of quarks and atoms dwarfed that of any of their teachers. He loved talking about duality, the fact that quantum entities existed as waves and particles at the same time.

"It's all infinite possibility," Jack loved to say. He thought anything was possible, like that his best friend might be carrying around cat food even though he didn't have a cat.

"Edward," Jack said.

Edward opened his eyes.

Jack knelt in front of him holding a scrawny black kitten. "Meet Faraday," Jack said in a quiet voice. "Faraday, this is Edward. He's okay. He's just a bit of a klutz. I suggest you stay away from his elbows."

The kitten was purring. He and Jack apparently had completed their bond.

Jack's head was bent, the kitten tucked under his broad chin. For a second, it was hard to see where the kitten's fur stopped and Jack's hair began. Jack's hair was as black as the kitten's fur.

Edward shifted his gaze from Jack to the kitten. "Hey, Faraday," he said. He held a finger in front of the kitten's tiny nose.

The kitten sniffed Edward's finger and kept purring.

"He might like you after all," Jack said.

"Um, is there a reason you've named a kitten that isn't yours?" Edward asked.

Jack shrugged. "He needs a name."

"Should we take him to the shelter?"

Jack shook his head. "No, I don't believe that would be best for him."

Faraday stopped purring. Jack murmured to him and scratched him behind the ears. "I think we should keep him," Jack said.

"My mom won't—"

"I know. Mine will, as long as we take care of him."

"We?"

"Well, *you* found him. You have to be one of his dads."

"I haven't exactly had a lot of role models for fatherhood."

"And I do?" Jack said.

"True."

Edward's dad left when Edward was three. He lived on the other side of the country with his second wife and three new kids. At Christmas and on Edward's birthday, he'd send a stupid card with twenty dollars inside. Jack's dad was still in the picture, but he was a long-haul trucker, and when he was home, all he wanted to do was watch sports, drink sodas, and eat junk food. He didn't understand Jack and had joked on more than one occasion that he wasn't convinced Jack was actually his son.

Another car went by. "Hey, freaks," some jerk shouted. "Forget the way home?"

Edward looked up and recognized a couple of the guys who lived up the street, both part of the group that played baseball in the streets in the summer. "Let's go," he said to Jack.

Jack held out Faraday. "You take him so I can get my books."

Edward gingerly accepted the furry bundle, tensing in expectation of a hiss or something worse. He wasn't used to animals. He liked them, but his mom never let him have one. He had no idea how to even hold a kitten, let alone how to take care of it.

Edward didn't think Jack knew, either. He sounded pretty confident about his mom letting him keep

Faraday, but the only pet he'd ever had was a goldfish he'd named Cousteau. Just a year ago, they'd had an hour-long memorial service after Jack found Cousteau floating upside down in his bowl. Edward had thought an hour-long service was excessive, but Jack pointed out that Cousteau had been alive longer than Jack and Edward (Jack's mom had bought Cousteau for Jack's nursery before he was born), so he deserved the appropriate respect.

Edward looked into Faraday's eyes. The kitten blinked at him. He gently stroked the cat's fur. It was dirty and felt stiff.

"Okay," Jack said. "Let's go."

"Where are we going? Home?"

"Let's go to the corner store and acquire food for him. Then we'll go to my house."

Edward nodded, and they headed down the block.

"Don't you think we should put up signs or something? What if someone is looking for it?" Edward asked.

"*It* is named Faraday, and I don't think anyone's been taking care of *him*."

"How do you know?"

"How do I know what? That no one is caring for him or that he is male?"

"Both."

"Well, the answer is the same: I had my hands on him. Feel how dirty and brittle his fur feels? He's been outside, and he's not getting good nutrition." Jack glanced at Faraday, who had relaxed into the crook of Edward's arm.

Edward could feel Faraday's quick heartbeat and the warmth of his tiny body against his own chest. There was something oddly calming about it.

"Well, I think we should put up signs," Edward said.

"Feel free to pursue your own agenda. My agenda is caring for our new cat."

True to Jack's prediction, his mom had no trouble with Faraday. This wasn't all that surprising. Mrs. Weston was a physics professor (which was why Jack couldn't be blamed for his obsession with duality), and if she wasn't in the classroom teaching, she was on her computer. "Publish or perish," she said whenever Edward commented on how hard she worked. Mrs. Weston wasn't all that aware of what was going on in the world beyond her work.

Jack's house had always been a mess when he was little. Now it was clean, but only because he cleaned it. He'd also taught himself to cook because he got tired of microwave dinners.

Now Jack was teaching himself how to take care of a cat.

Three weeks after they had found Faraday, he had not only settled into the Weston household, he was the boss of it, or at least the boss of Jack. Now the proud user of a state-of-the-art kitty litter station, a cat tower, and several cat beds, Faraday looked and acted like a very different critter than the one Edward and Jack had found.

Edward's posters had resulted in no calls about Faraday, and he was relieved about that. If the posters had led to someone taking Faraday away, he wasn't sure Jack would have forgiven him. And truthfully, Edward wouldn't have forgiven himself. He was in love with Faraday every bit as much as Jack was. This was why he now spent even more time at Jack's house.

"How come you and Jack never hang out here anymore?" his mother had asked the day before.

Edward had been trying to read the latest horror story by his favorite author. He answered her simply, "Faraday."

"What's a Faraday?" his mother reached out and snatched the book from his grasp.

Edward gritted his teeth, but he didn't say anything. His mom set down a bowl of chicken soup in front of him. He reached for the crackers, almost knocked his milk over, and caught it just in time. His mom gave him a look that he ignored.

"Don't you remember me telling you about the kitten we found? The one I made the posters for?" he asked her.

"Oh, sure. The kitten is called Faraday?"

Edward nodded and slurped his soup.

"Why?" his mom asked.

Edward explained about Michael Faraday and told her he was pretty sure the kitten was smart enough to develop some laws of electrochemistry on his own, if he had opposable thumbs. The kitten had an extraordinary ability to get whatever he wanted.

A case in point was happening right now.

Jack's dad had come home from his latest stretch on the road the night before. According to Jack, his dad had gone straight to bed and hadn't noticed the new addition to the household. Minutes before, however, he'd shuffled into the family room and flopped into his leather recliner. Reaching for the remote, his hand instead encountered a handful of kitten.

"What the hell?"

Jack and Edward, who had been sitting on the room's big brown rug using a laser pointer to amuse Faraday, froze. Jack flicked off the laser pointer. Faraday looked around, trying to find his missing prey. When he couldn't locate it, Faraday said, "Murrp?"

Jack was right about the variety of a kitten's sounds. Faraday had an extensive *language*, much of which Jack and Edward understood.

Murrp meant the exact same thing Mr. Weston had just said: "What the hell?" Or maybe Faraday's version was more colorful. Edward wasn't sure.

"Where'd the cat come from?" Mr. Weston asked as he popped open a can of soda. He set the soda next to a coaster Jack had ineffectually placed on the end table next to the recliner.

"We found him," Jack said, his usual smile wavering slightly. "Mom said we could keep him."

Edward was fascinated by how Jack's normal complex speech patterns became simple sentences when he spoke to his dad. Poor Jack. He tried to relate to his dad. It just didn't do much good.

"She did, huh?" Mr. Weston scowled.

Not only did Jack's dad not share Jack's personality or interests, he looked nothing like Jack. Mr. Weston was broad-shouldered and tall. His hair was black like Jack's, but his features were totally different. He had big features—large eyes, a broad nose, a jutting chin.

"What good is a cat?" Mr. Weston asked.

Faraday looked at Jack's dad and said, "Mawp." Then he stepped on the remote, right on the power button.

The TV came on. It was on a cooking channel.

Before Mr. Weston could reach for the remote to change the channel, Faraday flicked his tail and stepped on the remote again. The channel changed, and a college basketball game appeared on the screen.

Jack's dad looked from Faraday to the TV and back again. "Not bad, cat."

Faraday said, "Meep," and jumped off the end table. He knew when his work was done.

And that was apparently that. Mr. Weston settled in to enjoy the game, and Jack, Edward, and Faraday retreated to Jack's room.

The addition of Faraday to Jack's life required that Jack make a few adjustments to his room. First, of course, were the already mentioned kitty litter station, cat tower, and beds. Three beds to be exact . . . but technically, only one of them was a bed, the fluffy kind that was like a pouf with a hole in the middle for Faraday to sink into; the other two weren't exactly beds—one was a "sleeping cave," kind of like a soft igloo, and the other was a hammock.

In addition to these basic kitty accoutrements, Jack and Edward had spent the better part of the previous three weeks turning Jack's bedroom into a kitten play paradise. Putting their combined physics knowledge and Edward's fledgling interest in woodworking together, they built a series of platforms, ramps, and "kitty-ways" all over the walls of the room. The network of feline paths ran up over Jack's book-stuffed shelving, and then circled the room at a level just a foot or so below the ceiling. In addition to these thoroughfares, Edward and Jack built a series of chain reaction mechanisms designed to keep a feline occupied for hours.

Faraday loved all of this, but what he loved most was Edward and Jack. Faraday was not just a smart kitty; he was a social kitty. He liked playing group games like catch me if you can, keep-away (which usually involved him taking off with something the humans didn't want him to have), and hide-and-seek. Faraday was far too good at all three games. He quite often tried the patience of his keepers to the point that they wanted nothing to do with him, but that's when he'd pull out his superpower.

Faraday was, above all else, a cuddle master. Not

aloof like any cat Edward had heard about, Faraday loved to snuggle and be stroked. His purr power was off the charts.

Settled for the moment on Edward's lap, he had his purr cranked up to eleven. Jack sank into his desk chair and straightened his schoolbooks. He grinned at Edward. "Wasn't that the most exceptional display of empathic relation between human and feline you have ever witnessed?"

Edward stroked Faraday's back. Faraday raised his tail into the vaguely question-mark-shaped "happy" position and said, "Parrrrrble."

"It was pretty amazing," Edward said.

Speaking of amazing, the difference in the way Faraday felt between the day they found him and now was pretty remarkable. In just twenty-one days, Faraday had gone from bony and rough to soft and silky. Now perfectly filled out, Faraday was the picture of health, and his fur shined. Jack claimed this was because he used a little of his "product," some kind of glop that supposedly made your hair glossy, on Faraday. Edward wasn't sure you were supposed to use human hair products on cats, but he didn't say anything. Faraday didn't seem to be suffering in any way.

He rubbed under Faraday's chin. Faraday shoved his head against Edward's fingers and said, "Plurrrmf."

"I think we should implement a training program for him," Jack said.

Edward blinked. "Can you train a cat?"

"Of course. I found a book online. It's written by a woman who makes her living from a cat act that tours the country. I'm not sure I approve of using cats in such a blatantly self-interested entrepreneurial way, but her skills are impressive nonetheless."

"It's not total self-interest," Edward said. "I assume she uses the money to take care of her cats, too."

"A fair point."

"I'm up for training," Edward said. "What do we need to do?"

"According to the book, we'll start with simple suggestions and then move to more complex ones."

"Suggestions?"

"I object to the use of the word, *command*."

"Um, okay."

"Given his genius level," Jack said, gesturing at Faraday, "I'm sure he'll know a host of suggestions in no time."

"I'm sure."

Jack's prediction proved to be true. With six weeks remaining in the school year, after just three months of training, Faraday was turning into a kitty performer extraordinaire. When Jack or Edward said to Faraday, "Could you sit, please?" Faraday would sit upright in a look-at-me-aren't-I-handsome posture. If you said, "Could you please come here?" Faraday would trot over as happy as you please. "Please stay where you are, if you could," would freeze Faraday in place.

Similar polite requests could get Faraday to lie down, go and get something, wave his paw, slap a high five, roll over, spin in a circle, jump, leap through your arms, and bow. It was pretty awesome, Edward thought.

Now they were moving on to something akin to dog agility training. Out of space in Jack's room to build anything else, Jack and Edward asked his mother for permission to build an agility course for Faraday in the backyard. Because neither Mrs. nor Mr. Weston cared about the wild wooded area behind their house, she agreed.

They often played with Faraday in the backyard on sunny days. Because he'd never shown any interest in being anywhere Edward and Jack weren't, they were sure he was safe back there. "We'll never leave him outside to weather the elements or the wilds of the forest on his own," Jack had said the first time they went outside to chase Faraday around.

Edward agreed. He'd even been nervous about coming outside to play at all. The first time they'd done it had been in response to Mrs. Weston's complaint about "the racket" Faraday was making running all over the house.

Faraday was no longer kitten-sized, and though he was still a cuddle master, his longer limbs and extended body often got him into trouble. He was as prone to knocking things on the floor as Edward was. The only difference between Edward and Faraday was that no one was constantly telling Faraday to be careful.

On a warm day in early May, Edward carried several lengths of two-by-twelves into Jack's backyard. Surprisingly, Mr. Weston had helped Jack and Edward buy the lumber for their project. Edward theorized that Mr. Weston was thrilled his son had taken an interest in something "manly" like woodworking. Of course, no one told Mr. Weston that Edward would be doing all the building, and Mr. Weston didn't hang around long enough to find out. There was a baseball game on TV.

Edward could faintly hear the game through an open window at the back of Jack's house, but it was mostly drowned out by the neighbor's lawn mower. The smell of freshly mowed grass wafted over from next door and mixed with the musty smell of the wet earth in the Westons' untended yard.

"I am of the opinion that we should first demarcate our layout with chalk," Jack said when Edward showed him his plans for Faraday's agility course.

Edward shrugged. "That's fine."

As Edward carried lumber and old tires and tubing this way and that, he realized that Jack's chalk markings would be the extent of Jack's contribution to the project . . . that, and pointing here and there as he instructed Edward where to place various aspects of the course.

While Edward and Jack planned Faraday's agility course, Faraday prowled the yard, on the lookout for large leaves left over, unraked, from the fall. (They were the next best thing to a laser pointer.)

Occasionally, a hefty breeze would toss some leaves around, keeping Faraday well amused while Jack planned and Edward got to work.

In the weeks to come, Edward would wonder whether he'd missed some sign that afternoon, something to warn him of impending disaster. Was there a hint somewhere in the time they spent training Faraday? A whisper from the gods? Any inkling of a threat?

He often wasn't paying enough attention to the things he needed to, and the idea that he'd missed an important warning often kept him awake, wondering. Still, he could never pinpoint anything that would have alerted him to what was coming. And he supposed that was a good thing.

In every paradise, a serpent lurked. In Edward and Jack and Faraday's paradise, the serpent was a butterfly— a pretty, orange, fluttering monarch butterfly.

Edward spent hours studying butterflies after it happened. He wanted to know if the butterfly's appearance was a fluke or whether he should have been aware that butterflies were out and about. It so happened that May was indeed a normal time for butterflies. Monarchs, Edward learned during the terrible weeks after that day, lay their eggs in March and April. Their eggs hatch into larvae that grow into caterpillars, and then two weeks after that, the caterpillars find a nice sheltered place to start creating a chrysalis, from which the butterflies emerge. The first generation of monarchs only lives two to six weeks. They have a grand time eating during that short period, and then they die after laying eggs for the second generation of monarchs. It's that generation from which the evil emerged.

Edward wished he'd known more about butterflies. He liked to think there'd have been no way he and his best friends would have been outside if he'd known. But then, how would he have known that Faraday would think a butterfly was a colorful flying leaf?

Faraday spotted the butterfly before Edward or Jack did. As soon as he did, he started scampering after it, the same way he chased a leaf. At first, Edward and Jack thought Faraday's antics were amusing. It was like watching a ballet: the lithe, sleek black cat leaping gracefully; the weightless butterfly swooping and diving. The way Faraday's paws reached for the butterfly, batting the air, was adorable.

But then their cat romped around the corner into the front yard.

"Faraday, could you please come here?" Jack called as Faraday rounded the side of the house.

Faraday didn't come.

Jack repeated the "suggestion."

No Faraday.

Edward and Jack exchanged a look and both took off at the same time. They tore around the corner of the house, and they found Faraday at the front edge of the yard, happily cavorting with the butterfly.

"Faraday, come here!" Jack screamed, all concerns about commands gone.

Faraday acted as if he hadn't heard a thing.

Edward didn't bother to call Faraday. He just ran across the yard. Faraday wasn't paying attention to him, so Edward planned to scoop up the cat unawares and be done with the whole anxious moment.

But Faraday zigged when Edward zagged—right into the street.

"Faraday!" Jack and Edward screeched in unison.

Because of Edward's dash toward where Faraday had been, Jack was closer to Faraday when he went into the street. Jack wasn't particularly fast, but he moved at the speed of light that afternoon. His typical smile gone, his lips compressed in determination, he tore out into the street after the cat, and he leaped for Faraday just as a dump truck roared around the corner and accelerated toward cat and boy.

"Stop!" Edward yelled.

He wasn't sure who he was yelling at. The truck's driver? Faraday? Jack?

The only one who seemingly listened to him was the truck's driver.

As Edward raced toward the street to rescue his friends, the truck's driver hit his brakes. The tires squealed, but the truck was going too fast to stop in time.

"No!" Edward wailed as the truck plowed right into and then over both Jack and Faraday.

Frozen, Edward stared at Jack's and Faraday's contorted bodies. He didn't step forward to see if they were alive. Both lay with their necks at an odd angle, their eyes open . . . but vacant.

Edward stumbled back, turned, and threw up in the gutter. Then his legs gave way, and he crumpled to the asphalt. He was strangely aware of the lawn mower droning on next door, but he couldn't hear anything else. The driver was out of his cab, on his phone. Someone from across the street was running forward, mouth open as if yelling. But all that was blurry and muted. The only thing Edward could see clearly was what was left of Jack and Faraday, and all he could do was sit in the street and stare into the unseeing eyes of his two best friends.

Although Edward's mother let him stay home for a few days, she forced him to go to school for the last two weeks of the year. He went . . . like a zombie. He easily finished his coursework, and he went home, relieved beyond words when school let out. His plan for the summer was to get in bed and stay there forever.

His mother tolerated Edward's withdrawal for a couple weeks after school ended, but then she started nagging him to get out of the house and "do something to take his mind off things." Like that was possible. Edward's mind was no longer his own. It was stuck in an endless time loop, one that replayed the worst moment of his life over and over and over again.

He kept seeing it in his mind's eye: happy Faraday frolicking into the street, panicked Jack running faster than he'd ever run before, both getting plowed over by the truck. Edward's ears kept playing the soundtrack of the moment over and over, the screech of the tires, the *thud* of the impact. A dull, wet crunching sound when Jack hit the pavement. A deep, rasping wail that split the world open when Jack's father came outside. Edward couldn't take his mind off what was indelibly etched there.

Edward was no longer in the universe he had lived in for all but a few months of his life. The Jack-and-Edward universe had collapsed in on itself. Edward had been sucked out of it and spewed unceremoniously into this nasty dimension where he was utterly and completely alone . . . well, except for his mom.

His mom now sat at the end of his bed fussing with the ubiquitous strands of hair that refused to cooperate with her hairdo. She looked around his messy room.

Edward watched the tendons in his mother's neck tighten as she gazed at the piles of dishes on both his desk and the floor. Her attention shifted to the mountain of books next to his bed. Desperate to escape the time loop, he'd been obsessively rereading every science-fiction book he owned. He'd pull a book down, read it, then toss it on the floor. His bookshelves were nearly bare. His floor was not.

His mom turned to look at him. Her nose twitched, and he knew why. He hadn't showered or changed out of pj's since school had ended.

"Edward, I know you're grieving," his mom began, "but . . ."

He looked at her blankly.

She swallowed and cleared her throat. "Do you want to talk to someone?"

Edward shook his head. Who would he talk to?

"I mean someone like a therapist?" his mom tried.

"No!" The word erupted from his mouth before he even knew he was going to say it. The idea of talking to some total stranger about his pain made him feel even sicker than he already did.

"Okay," his mom said quickly. "Okay." She touched his knee. "I just . . . I just don't know how to help you."

"The only thing that will help me is bringing them back."

His mom frowned, and her eyes filled with tears. "I'm so sorry." She swallowed and looked away from him. "If only you two hadn't found that stupid cat."

"Faraday wasn't stupid!" Edward shouted. He clenched his fists in the fabric of his space-patterned bedspread. His hand bunched up a bright purple whirl-pool galaxy.

"Faraday was the best cat ever!" Edward screamed at his mother. "Better than most people!" His volume increased even more, and he felt spittle fly from his mouth. "I'm glad we found him. He was the only friend I've ever had besides Jack!" Edward's chest heaved. He struggled to breathe.

"Oh, Edward," his mother said. She got up and moved to his side, wrapping him in a tight bear hug that made breathing even harder.

He didn't struggle to get free, though. He was sobbing now.

His mother began rocking them back and forth. He let her. "I'm sorry," she whispered in his ear. "I'm so sorry. I didn't mean what I said. I feel terrible that you're hurting this way. I hate to see you like this."

Edward felt the tension begin to recede from his body. He relaxed into his mom's arms, but he didn't say anything. He wasn't ready to forgive her for what she'd said.

Ever since Jack and Faraday . . . since they . . . Edward hated even thinking the word—*died*—both Edward's mom and Jack's mom had been blaming the whole thing on Faraday. Mrs. Weston now called Faraday "that evil cat."

He hated her for blaming Faraday. It wasn't Faraday's fault.

Whose fault was it?

Edward thought the fault was shared. For sure, the butterfly was at fault. If the butterfly hadn't gone into the street, Faraday wouldn't have gone into the street. If Faraday hadn't gone into the street, Jack wouldn't have gone into the street.

The driver, the police said, was going twenty miles per hour over the speed limit; the tire's skid marks proved that. So, obviously, the driver was somewhat at fault. Edward's mom said the police were charging the driver with vehicular manslaughter.

Edward thought the Westons were at fault, too. They were the ones who said Faraday was too "rambunctious" to play in the house all the time.

Maybe the woman who wrote the cat training book was at fault. If she hadn't written that book, he and Jack would never have thought to build an agility course for Faraday.

And, of course, he and Jack were at fault, too. If they had been paying more attention, if they'd gone after Faraday faster when he went around the corner, if they hadn't been so cocky about training Faraday and being so sure Faraday would follow their "suggestions" . . . If, if, if.

But what good did it do to assign fault? It didn't change the outcome.

Edward's mom let him go. She kissed his forehead and wrinkled her nose.

"I have to go to work. Will you be okay?"

He looked at the lines bunched up between her eyes. He thought there might be more lines there than there were before . . . well . . . *before.*

"I'll be okay," he told her.

She pulled back and studied him for several seconds. Then she stood. "Maybe you could take a shower." She winked at him.

Edward gave her a half smile. "I was trying to set a smelliest human record."

She smiled back. "Hmm. Well, I don't think you have far to go to achieve that."

"Actually," Edward said, "there's this sixty-five-year-old guy in India who's gone thirty-seven years without washing. For a while everyone thought he was the world's smelliest man, but then they found this Iranian dude who hasn't washed in sixty years. He's eighty years old and hates water, eats lots of smelly meat—his favorite is porcupine—and he puts animal, um, dung in his pipe."

"You're making that up." His mom's eyes were wide, and her lip was curled.

"No, really. I read it in a couple different places."

His mom ruffled his hair, and for some reason, it didn't bother him this time. He grinned at her.

"Well," she said, "you're going to fail at the record. Because if you haven't showered by the end of the day, pizza is a thing of the past."

Edward gave his mom a look of mock horror. "No pizza?!"

She smiled at him and stood. She hesitated. "You'll call me if you need me?"

"Sure."

Edward realized that for a few seconds, when he was talking about the smelliest men, he'd forgotten to be sad. He felt a little bad about that. How could he let himself get distracted from his sadness? Jack and Faraday were more important than smelly men.

His mom studied Edward for another few seconds,

then took a deep breath and left his room. He listened to her head down the short hall. He heard her jingle her keys and snap her purse shut. Then he heard the *shush*, the tap of her walk, the friction of her stockings, and the sound of her high heels.

"I'll come home for lunch," she called out.

"Okay," he shouted back.

The front door opened and closed with a squeak and a thump. He sat in the silence and listened to the sound of his mom's car engine sputter to life before roaring once and then settling into a quiet purr as she put it into gear.

The purr reminded him of Faraday.

He slumped down against his pillows and pulled his bedspread up over his head. Under the covers, he breathed slowly in and out. He liked it under here. He'd spent a lot of time under here in the last several weeks. It was kind of like a deprivation chamber, or as close to it as he could get. All he could hear was the sound of his inhale and exhale, and when he focused on that sound, he forgot to notice the sensations of the covers rubbing against his skin, the support of the mattress beneath him. He also forgot to notice the sour smell of his breath and his body odor. He went into a sort of nothing state. In this state, he could get the mental replay to freeze for a few seconds. But then it would start up again . . . like it was now.

Edward threw off the bedspread. He inhaled . . . and immediately regretted it. How did those old guys stand themselves? He'd only gone two weeks without washing, and he wanted to drop-kick himself into the nearest bathtub.

Sighing, Edward got out of his bed. He needed to take a shower.

When Edward returned to his bedroom after a very long, very hot, very soapy shower, the contrast between his newly washed state and the smell of the stale air in his room was more than he could stand. He picked his way around all the cascading mountains of books to get to his window. Opening the shade let in so much sun that his eyes watered, so he only left the shade open long enough to lift the window. Then he pulled the shade again. He wanted fresh air. He wasn't ready for light.

A warm breeze caught the vinyl shade and flicked it back and forth against the window frame, causing a *whoosh-click* every few minutes. Edward ignored the sound and looked around his room.

How many hours had Edward and Jack spent in this room? Maybe he should sit down and calculate that. Reading science fiction didn't seem to be enough to distract his mind from the nightmare he was replaying. Maybe a complicated math problem would do the trick.

Edward crossed to his desk, opened a drawer, and took out a pad of paper, a pencil, and his calculator. He looked at the edges of his antique walnut desk. His mom had bought that desk for him when he and Jack had started junior high. Jack had been jealous of it because it was so big. Jack's desk was a spindly thing made up of particle board covered with wood veneer. He said it didn't nurture his brain cells. So, Edward had let Jack use his desk most afternoons. Jack had done a lot of his homework in the previous two years at this desk. Edward had done his on his bed.

Edward wiped his eyes and turned away from the desk. He needed to add more dishes to the pile so he could barely see the desk at all. He set down the paper, pencil, and calculator on his bed, piled more dishes on the desk, and turned away from those memories.

He wandered over to his shelves. Only a few books remained there. His least favorites. They lay limply in the layers of dust that had hidden behind the other books. He sighed and returned to his bed.

Plopping on the bed, he picked up his pad of paper. Okay. How many hours was Jack in this room?

Before they rescued Faraday, he and Jack had split their time pretty equally between Jack's room and his. So, all he had to do was figure the total hours they'd spent together and divide it in half. He began to try to find his earliest memory of Jack. That was easy.

It was right after Christmas, when he was only two. Edward's dad had gotten him a huge set of building blocks, so he and Jack had built a massive castle. Then Edward decided to be a dragon. He threw his arms out to create dragon wings, and he flung his hand into one of the uppermost blocks. This started a slow-motion disintegration of all their efforts. In a matter of seconds, the blocks went from castle to pile of rubble. As it did, Jack threw up his little arms, smiled, and shouted, "Earthcake!"

Edward felt something drip from his chin, and he realized he was crying. He dropped his pad of paper and wiped his face.

This wasn't working. He couldn't tally up the hours he and Jack were together without remembering the times they'd shared. He wasn't ready to do that.

He looked at his empty shelves again. He needed more books.

But to get them, he'd have to go to the library. Forget that. He wasn't leaving the house.

That left him with TV. Edward sighed, exited his room, and went down the hall to the living room at the front of the house.

The living room smelled like the lemon dusting spray his mom used. That wasn't bad. It was better than the smell of his bedroom.

The problem with the living room was that it was too bright. The blue-sky day outside the house was shoving its way into the room. Edward shrank back into the hall as he watched some kids in the street bike past. He winced at the sound of a car whooshing by. That was a sound he wished he never had to hear again.

Edward thought about returning to his room, but too many memories and not enough books waited for him there. The TV was his only hope for continued sanity.

Taking a deep breath, Edward crossed the rug to the beige sofa that sat under a picture window. The window's drapes were open. He crossed to the drawstring and pulled the drapes closed. The heavy maroon drapes were thermal, room darkening. So, once he'd closed them, the room was like a cave. Not only was the light blocked out, the outside sounds were muted. That was better.

Edward plopped on the sofa and grabbed the remote.

After a few minutes of channel surfing, Edward settled on an episode of an old sci-fi series, which thankfully held his attention until the commercial. When a commercial for some "amazing" cleaning product came on, he muted the TV and thought about getting up to get a bag of chips from the kitchen. He started to stand, but then the cleaning product ad disappeared, and a new one took over the screen.

On a black-and-white-checkerboard backdrop, big red words flashed across the screen: GRIEVING THE LOSS OF A BELOVED PET?

Edward froze and stared at the TV.

The image of a large, cartoonish brown bear wearing a top hat filled the screen. The bear was talking. Edward quickly unmuted the TV as the words FAZBEAR ENTERTAINMENT PRESENTS FAZBEAR FRIENDLY FACES! scrolled beneath the bear.

"Just send in a few strands of hair from your lost pet, and let Fazbear Entertainment do the rest! We use your pet's DNA to craft a face that looks exactly like your beloved furry friend. The face is then integrated onto an animatronic body to create a loyal pet that will follow you around forever."

The image on the screen shifted to an example of the Friendly Face, and Edward watched in awe as a robotic orange cat romped around after the red dot of a laser pointer.

"What a small price to pay to feel joy again rather than wallow in those sad feelings of loss and longing." The bear looked like he was talking directly to Edward, and Edward could feel the intensity of the bear's cool blue eyes.

On the screen, more red writing flashed: FOR A LIMITED TIME ONLY: AN AMAZING DEAL JUST FOR YOU!

The bear started talking again. "And, if you order within the next thirty minutes, you'll get *free shipping*!"

A price streaked across the screen. It was a lot, at least for Edward, but he thought he had enough in his savings stash.

The bear leaned forward, making his communication feel even more personal, almost intimate. "If you don't love your Friendly Face," the bear said, "then my name isn't Freddy Fazbear." The bear leaned back and smiled, flashing a wide mouthful of teeth. It pointed at its chest, "And I *am* Freddy Fazbear, so you're guaranteed to be thrilled with your new faithful friend!"

The robotic cat reappeared on the screen, and Freddy's voice-over said, "What better way to

memorialize a precious friend than with a new pal—
someone who will remind you of the memories you
made with your pet while helping to make new ones,
together. Why settle for an urn full of ashes or a photo
on a wall when you can have a memorial you can play
with, one who will keep you company any time you
want?"

More red letters erupted onto the screen: GET YOUR
FRIENDLY FACE TODAY! CALL NOW!

CALL NOW! faded out, to be replaced by a large red
phone number.

Edward looked around wildly for something to write
on. Of course, there was nothing. His mother kept
the living room too neat. Frantically, he read the phone
number twice, and then he began chanting the numbers
in his head.

He got up and ran to the kitchen. He grabbed the
notepad his mom kept next to the phone. As he pulled
it toward him, he knocked the phone off the counter.
He didn't even try to grab it. It hit the floor with a *crack*
as he scribbled down the number before he forgot it.

Edward pulled out one of the chairs from under the
kitchen table. He sat and stared at the phone number.
In the living room, a woman screamed on the TV. The
sci-fi show was back on. He didn't care—if this worked
out, he wouldn't need escapism anymore.

He smiled at the phone number. For the first time in
weeks, it didn't feel like a monster was trying to squeeze
the heart out of Edward's chest. He suddenly saw a

sliver of hope for his future. Maybe he could have a friend after all.

Edward nodded to himself. He was going to order a Friendly Face, and then it would be kind of like Jack was still here. As long as Edward had a robotic Faraday, he could pretend his friend was around.

He stood and reached for the phone. It wasn't there. "Oh right," he muttered. He looked down at the floor and grimaced. The phone had a crack in the receiver. His mother wasn't going to be happy with him.

He turned the phone on and heard the dial tone. Well, at least it still worked. Edward smiled and punched in the number he'd written down.

By the time Edward had talked to the nice lady at Fazbear Entertainment and was given the address to which he should send his money and the hair of his lost pet, it was mid-afternoon. He needed to get moving.

Now he was pedaling his bike along the sidewalk, just a few houses down from Jack's house. He had a lump in his throat, and the closer he got to the two-story brick house where his friend had lived, the bigger the lump got.

Jack's street was only a couple blocks from Edward's. Like the street Edward lived on, Jack's street was lined with a mix of older homes that ranged from quaint Craftsman cottages like the one Edward and his mom lived in to big Tudor and tall Victorian places. All the homes were guarded by ancient oak and walnut trees, some fronted by tall hedges. Others had picket or wrought-iron fences. If only Jack's house had had a fence.

The street was pretty quiet. Edward heard a few little kids squealing from behind one of the houses. In the distance, a radio played an upbeat pop tune. The music felt all wrong. It should have been slow and dark, something in a minor key.

When Edward reached the corner right before Jack's house, he stopped his bike and leaned it against the massive trunk of an oak tree in the yard next to Jack's. He stood on shaky legs and swallowed hard before he looked at the street.

The street was empty, but in Edward's mind, it wasn't. He began to breathe heavily.

What was in Edward's mind got bigger and brighter, and suddenly, it seemed to jump out of his head and explode into the street as if he was watching the whole scene, once again, in real time. There was Faraday gleefully batting at the butterfly. There was Jack, his face stretched into a contorted expression of dread. There was the truck—

Edward leaned over and concentrated on breathing. He had to get this over with.

Straightening, Edward darted out into the street. He didn't even look for cars, he realized after he was in the street; he just ran.

He trotted to the place where Jack and Faraday lay. He could see them there. It was a weird projection from his mind, he knew, but they looked real, disturbingly real.

Because he could see them, he knew exactly where to find some of Faraday's fur. When he got there, though, he realized he wouldn't have needed his mind's upsetting reenactment. A bloodstain marked the spot of Jack's and Faraday's last seconds on earth. When Edward saw it, he had to clamp his mouth shut to keep from spewing what was left of his undigested soup all over the street.

Wanting this over with, Edward spastically scanned the area around the bloodstain for black hair. Finally, he spotted some lying at the end of the rust-colored splotch. Pulling a plastic bag from his pocket, Edward quickly leaned over, plucked the hair from the road, and dropped it into the bag. Then he ran back to his bike, jumped on, and pedaled away as fast as he could. He was home just a few minutes later.

Tearing into his house, Edward slammed the door and leaned against it, panting.

Okay. The hard part is done. Just two more things to do, and they're easy.

Edward hurried into his mother's home office, perfectly neat and decorated in creams and pale blues. He went to the pine storage armoire in the corner of the room and dug inside it for a small padded envelope and some stamps.

He took both of these back to the kitchen, and put his money and the plastic bag of Faraday's hair inside the envelope. He added the right postage, and after checking the time, he went back outside to his bike and headed to the post office.

The lady at Fazbear Entertainment had told Edward it would take eight weeks for his Friendly Face to get to him. Eight weeks! That was a long time. But it was better than being forever without Faraday and Jack.

Of course, he knew that his Friendly Face could not and would not replace Jack and Faraday, but he believed that having an animated reminder of the kitten that he and his best friend had so loved would help him start wanting to live again. Because right now, he really didn't care too much about life.

Edward marked his calendar with the approximate date on which he expected his Friendly Face to arrive: August 28. Every day, he crossed out a square and told himself he was one step closer to having what he was waiting for.

The summer was long and lonely.

Edward's mother suggested that he go to a camp, but he flatly refused. She threatened to put him in summer school. "You like to learn," she coaxed.

He shook his head. "If you enroll me, I'll run away from home."

"I'll find you if you do that."

"I read a lot, Mom," Edward said. "I've read a lot about going off the grid, too. I won't be easy to locate."

His mother just shook her head and went to work.

When Edward's mother began talking about moving to a different town for a fresh start, Edward realized he'd better do something to prevent such a drastic action.

"Will you take me to the library tomorrow to get some books?" he asked her over a Sunday breakfast of overcooked French toast. His mom wasn't stellar in the kitchen, but most of what she made was edible.

"Sure!" she said. The eagerness in her voice made him feel bad. She was thinking that he was "snapping out of it."

He wasn't.

Day after day crawled by. Finally, August 28 came . . . and went.

No package.

Edward called Fazbear Entertainment. "Where's my Friendly Face?" he asked another nice lady on the phone.

"Could you give me your name, dear?"

"Edward Colter."

He listened to keyboard clicking through the phone line.

"Here you are," she sang out after a moment. "There was a delay in manufacturing because of a production anomaly. We're so sorry for your inconvenience, but you should have your Friendly Face in about two weeks. We'll include a discount coupon for another Fazbear Entertainment order as an apology for the delay."

Edward sighed. He didn't want any other Fazbear Entertainment stuff. He wanted his robotic Faraday.

Now he was going to have to go back to school before his animatronic cat arrived. Somehow that made returning to school even more depressing than it already was.

But what could he do except wait?

So, he waited.

Two weeks into his new school year, two weeks of being studiously avoided by every one of his classmates, two weeks of being babied by the high school teachers who'd been informed of May's "tragedy," and Edward was trying to get used to being a freshman without his friend by his side. Every day was an exercise in endurance, just getting through the long hours until he could go home and check his mail.

Finally, on a Monday afternoon, he arrived home to find a package waiting for him on the front porch. "Yes!" he shouted before snatching it up and taking it inside.

Edward dropped his backpack on the floor right inside the door. His mom hated when he did that, but he'd pick it up later. He ran into the kitchen with his package. Setting the big cardboard box with the Fazbear Entertainment logo on the counter, Edward hurried to the knife block by the stove and pulled out a paring knife. A gust of wind outside rattled the small paned window over the sink. He glanced out. The black clouds he'd noticed overhead during his bus ride home from school were churning low in the sky. They were in for a storm.

He didn't care. Turning his back on the window, he returned to the kitchen table.

Outside, a dog barked incessantly, almost frenziedly, so much so that if Edward hadn't been in a hurry to open his package, he'd have checked on it. Other than the crazy dog, it was quiet. The only sound inside the house was the low hum of the refrigerator.

Edward began carefully slicing along the seal of the Fazbear Entertainment box. The seal was black and white checked, like the background in the commercial he'd seen. It had Freddy Fazbear stickers spaced every few inches as well. He felt kind of bad slicing through Freddy's toothy smile.

The knife made a chuffing sound as it sawed through the cardboard. Edward's breath came in excited little gasps that joined the knife's rhythm.

Edward didn't bother to cut the tape at the ends of the box. He just grabbed both sides of the lid and yanked, tearing the tape with a *snap*. Taking a deep breath, he flipped back the lid and started digging through the Styrofoam peanuts that covered his prize.

The peanuts flew as he reached through them. They snowed all over the table and the floor. Edward ignored them and also the small instruction booklet he found in the peanuts. He could see black hair on the body of a medium-sized cat. He was almost shaking in anticipation of meeting his new robotic pal. Digging out more

Styrofoam, he got a grip on his new Friendly Face. Then he pulled it from the box in a spray of more peanuts that skittered this way and that.

Edward lifted the Friendly Face from the box and held it up before his eyes.

Edward screamed and dropped the Friendly Face. It landed on its legs in the open box, and the Styrofoam peanuts held it upright before Edward's appalled gaze.

He staggered a couple steps back from the table. *What had he done?*

Edward could hear his mother's voice in his head: "Edward, you have to be more careful!"

How many times had she told him that his single-minded focus would get him in trouble? How many accidents had he had to clean up because he wasn't thinking about what he was doing? How many times had he messed up in school, making him the butt of endless jokes?

The day Edward had shot into the street to pluck hair from the pavement, the only thing he'd been thinking about was being done with his disgusting task so he could send off his order for his Friendly Face. He hadn't been really looking at what he was doing. He hadn't examined the hair he'd gathered to make sure it was *cat* hair. He'd just scraped up the first black hair he'd seen, and he'd taken off.

And this is what he got for it.

Sitting in front of Edward, perched on top of a mound of Styrofoam peanuts like a deformed king, the body of a robotic cat was attached to the stiff, powder-white face of . . . Jack.

Not Faraday.

Jack.

Instead of Faraday's sweet, furry face—the face Edward had expected to see when he'd opened the box—the human hairs Edward had sent in had resulted in the stark white mold of a dead-looking human face. Jack's face.

On the hard material, Jack's brown eyes were motionless, but they appeared to be gazing intelligently at Edward, just waiting for Edward to say something so Jack could reply with his usual affected display of esoteric knowledge. Edward struggled to breathe as he stared at Jack's slightly flat nose, thick lips turned up in a smile, and his broad chin. These were Jack's features . . . attached to an animatronic cat.

It was an abomination.

Edward felt sick.

Using the back of his hand to knock the Friendly Face out of the way, Edward dumped the remainder of the Styrofoam peanuts from the box. He looked at the empty box and the thing that was part his friend and part cat robot; then he wildly surveyed the kitchen. Spotting a wooden spoon in the pottery jar by the stove, which his mother used for her cooking utensils, he rushed over and grabbed it. He then picked up the box and held its opening level with the kitchen table. He used the spoon to shove the awful—what? creature? machine?—into the box.

He knew he was acting crazy, but he didn't want to touch the thing. It was just too creepy, too . . . *wrong*.

Once he got the nasty Friendly Face in the box, he pushed the instructions manual into the box as well. He didn't even want to look at the manual. He had no intention of activating this thing.

He looked around again. He had to get rid of it.

He didn't want to just throw it away. First, if he did that, his mom could find it. Second, the garbage was far too easy to get out of.

Edward gasped and took two steps away from the table. Why had he just thought that?

He shook his head. He didn't want to ponder the morbid place from which that thought had arisen. He'd read way too many horror stories and science-fiction novels, watched too many macabre movies.

He was being ridiculous, of course. But he still wasn't going to throw this thing in the trash. No. He was going to bury it.

Outside, thunder rumbled. He glanced out the window. The sky was still roiling. He'd have to hurry.

Grabbing the box, taking care not to touch what was inside, Edward hurried out the back door of the kitchen. He scurried to the garden shed at the rear of the yard. With fumbling fingers, he turned the dial of the combination lock. It took three tries before he got the numbers to line up right so he could get the lock open.

Finally, he was able to get into the shed. He grabbed

a shovel and trotted to the perimeter of the yard, right up against the fence at the edge of the property. If he could have taken the Friendly Face someplace *off* his property, he would have. He wanted it far away, but he needed the thing buried *now*. He had no way to transport it, and even if he did, the storm clouds were about to release their burden. He didn't really want to be outside in a thunderstorm.

So he started digging.

He'd dug a two-foot diameter hole about a foot down when he saw a streak of lightning out of the corner of his eye. Even though his hands smarted, he dug even faster. In only a few more minutes, he had the hole deep enough.

Running back to the deck, Edward grabbed the box, then returned, even faster, to the hole he'd dug. The skies overhead grumbled loudly. A drop of rain landed on his nose.

Edward dumped the contents of the box into the hole. The manual hit the dirt first. The Friendly Face landed on the manual, faceup. Edward groaned when the rigid version of his friend's smiling features looked up at him. He tossed aside the box and began shoveling dirt into the hole at a breakneck pace. Every clod of dirt that hit the Jack face made him flinch. He felt like he was burying his friend alive. He could have sworn the Jack face, though wearing Jack's nonstop smile, looked accusatory.

Ignoring the condemnation in the fake Jack face,

Edward shoveled until the white was obscured and finally covered completely. Stamping down the dirt once he had it all over the hole, he wasn't happy with the slight mound that was left, but he hoped the rain might pound the dirt down enough for it to settle in and around the Friendly Face.

A couple more drops hit Edward. With sore, dirty hands, he grabbed the empty box and the shovel. He darted into the shed, put the shovel where it belonged, and tucked the box behind a few other empty boxes his mother saved "just in case." He'd get rid of it later.

He barely got the door closed and the lock clicked into place before the rain started coming down in heavy sheets. By the time he was back in the kitchen, he was soaked. When he went inside, he left mud and water all over the kitchen floor.

He glanced at the clock over the phone. He had just an hour before his mom would be home. He had to hurry if he was going to dispose of the Styrofoam peanuts and clean up the floor before she got here.

Even though Edward was now thirteen, his mom still came into his room to kiss him good night. That usually bugged him, but tonight, her fussing was welcome. Edward was so rattled by the awful Friendly Face that he was having trouble slowing his breathing.

The weather wasn't helping. Outside his window, the storm that had begun just as he finished burying the Jack-cat-robot-thing was now slamming into the house like an army storming a castle. Every clap of thunder sounded like the *thwack* of a catapult being loosed upon a fortress. Every blanket of rain that rattled against the side of the house sounded like a spray of arrows beating down on the poor beleaguered inhabitants of the stronghold. That was how Edward saw himself and his mother—two defenseless commoners huddled against the onslaught of the enemy, unable to defend themselves.

All evening, Edward recoiled every time the thunder boomed. After the third time, he pulled into himself, like a turtle hiding in its shell. His mom said, "Edward, what in the world? You've never been afraid of thunder before."

"It's not the thunder," he said.

"Then what is it?" Her hair was down for the evening. It hung around her face, making her look much younger and friendlier than she did when she had it up for work. She peered at him as if she could figure out what was going on with him by looking hard enough.

He shook his head. "It's nothing. I'm just being weird."

"You're not weird," his mom said.

Edward laughed. "I thought you lawyers had some code that didn't let you lie."

His mom smiled. "That's true, but I am allowed to bend the truth a bit. You're not weird. You're unique."

Edward laughed again. Then the rain pummeled the

windows once more. He jumped up. "I think I'll go to bed early."

Now, at his bedside, his mom felt his forehead. "You feel a little hot. You might have a fever. Maybe that's why the storm is bothering you this evening."

Edward shrugged. "Maybe." It wasn't exactly a lie. He just might have a fever, and it could be adding to the trepidation that sat on his chest like a gargoyle.

"Do you want me to take your temperature?" his mom asked.

"I'm not a baby," Edward said. "I can take it myself. But I'd rather go to sleep now."

His mom pressed her lips together, then nodded. She leaned over and kissed his cheek.

"I love you, kiddo."

"Love you, too, Mom."

His mom gave him one last look, walked to the door, turned off the light, and left the room.

Edward wasn't ready to close his eyes, so he blinked and let his eyes adjust to the near dark. As soon as they did, he could make out the various items in his room. Enough light came in under the door from the hallway to illuminate the outline of his desk, still mostly buried under a pile of clothes he refused to move, and the sharp contours of his shelves. A small night-light on the other side of the room cast a glow that lit up his bulletin board just enough to remind him of the photos he still couldn't bring himself to look at, nor take down.

Edward felt as stiff as a corpse.

He groaned. Now why did he have to compare himself to a corpse? What was wrong with him? Why was he letting the Friendly Face bother him so much? It was just a stupid toy that went wrong.

He shuddered and pulled the covers up to his chin. Or was it?

The problem was it *wasn't* just a toy. It was something designed to be animated, something that contained his dead friend's DNA. He didn't want to think about the thousand and one ways that could be bad.

"Stop it!" Edward hissed at himself.

He needed an imaginotomy, or whatever they might call it if one's imagination could be cut away from a person's mind. His was way too sinister tonight.

Edward forced himself to close his eyes. He concentrated on a logic problem from math class . . . and eventually, he relaxed enough to fall asleep.

Edward sat up in his bed. He was perfectly still. He listened.

Something had awakened him.

But what?

Outside, rain still drummed on the roof. The thunder was so loud and so powerful that each reverberation made the house shake. Was that what had yanked him out of sleep?

He frowned and kept listening. He didn't think so. The sound that disturbed him hadn't been an ordinary sound. And it hadn't been a loud sound. It had been a subtle sound, a sinuous and sly sort of sound. Something like a pattering, but not a friendly pattering like the rain.

Edward reached over and turned on the small brass lamp that sat on his oak nightstand. As soon as he rotated the switch, a bolt of lightning lit up the shade pulled over his window, and his nightstand light went out. So did his night-light.

The storm had taken out the power. Great. That was just great.

Edward felt around in the dark and pulled open his nightstand drawer. He grabbed his flashlight and turned it on.

Hesitating to see if he could talk himself out of believing he'd heard something, Edward failed to do so and forced himself to get out of bed. He listened intently, concentrating on peeling back the auditory layers of the storm so he could hear whatever was skulking under those more assertive sounds.

What had he heard?

Edward shone his light this way and that as he crossed his room. Nothing was out of place.

When he reached his door, he cautiously opened it. He peered out and pointed the beam of his flashlight down the hallway.

The hall was empty.

Edward tiptoed down the hall and aimed his light into the living room. It looked perfectly normal.

From behind his mom's closed door, he heard snoring. She was a heavy sleeper.

Edward continued his tour of the house, checking in his mom's home office, in the bathroom, and in the kitchen. Nothing was out of place.

He returned to his room, got in bed, and turned out his flashlight.

As soon as he lay his head back on the pillow, he heard a creak.

Edward stiffened. Had he imagined that?

If he hadn't imagined it, did it mean something was in the house?

Something?

Why did he think *something*? Wouldn't it be more reasonable to think *someone*?

Reasonable, sure. Accurate? He didn't think so.

He waited, again trying to listen past the storm.

A faint scrape came from outside his door.

Edward flipped on his flashlight again. He shined it at his door, spotlighting the doorknob. All the slowly turning doorknob scenes in every creepy movie he'd ever watched started running through his mind, and by the time he'd gone through just a few of them, he could have sworn *his* doorknob was turning as well. But was it?

Wanting nothing more than to hide under his bed, close his eyes, and cover his ears, Edward took a deep breath and threw back the covers. Keeping his gaze on his doorknob, which didn't seem to be moving at all—did it?—he crept across his room, leaned against his door, and listened.

Rain continued to batter the house. Between blasts of wind, thunder detonated, always just a second or so after the room blazed bright for an instant; the lightning was hitting close by. Between the rain's thrum and the thunder's bellows, Edward had trouble picking out any other sounds. But wait, there, what was that?

He frowned, pushed harder against the door, and concentrated. Had he imagined that sound?

No. There it was again. It was a chittering sound, something like metal tapping on wood, only really fast. Or like marbles cascading down a metal tube. What *was* that?

Edward gripped his flashlight hard and opened his door.

His flashlight was pretty bright—2,400 lumens—so he was able to brighten the entire hall when he aimed the light straight ahead. The hall was, as it had been before, empty.

He swung the light toward the opening to the living room. Shadows from beyond the opening hunched in wait for him. He listened for another few seconds, and when he heard the sound again—was it more skittering than chittering?—he tentatively moved toward the living room.

As he went, his light and his head swiveled this way and that. Why couldn't he tell where the sound was coming from?

It had to be the storm. The cacophony outside was disrupting his ears' ability to pinpoint direction. For one second, he thought the sound was coming from behind his mother's door. But no, that was just her bed creaking when she turned over in her sleep . . . he was pretty sure. The next second, he thought the sound originated in the living room. But when he stepped into that room and shone his light right, left, and center, he saw nothing out of place. Then he heard the sound again, and it seemed to be coming from just inside the back door.

He slunk into the kitchen, then quickly aimed his light at the door. It was closed tight, the dead bolt in the right position. He heard a click and shot his light to the left. Nothing. It must have been the refrigerator.

Shaking his head at his paranoia, Edward muttered, "Just go back to bed and make like an opossum, would you?"

As he retreated back to his room, retracing his steps through the living room, his light still spastically searching for the source of the odd sounds, he idly wondered whether opossums had overactive imaginations like his. This nonsensical query gave him a few seconds of relief from the tension turning his muscles into coils ready to snap at just the slightest—

A *pfft, pfft, pfft* came from right behind him.

Edward whirled.

His light jittered into every inky crevice of the living room. It found nothing unusual.

By now, Edward's breath was coming in little puffs. He was just one more sound away from screaming his head off. He couldn't take this much longer.

Edward scuttled down the hall, dashed into his room, and yanked the door shut behind him. He pointed the flashlight all over his room. It was just as he'd left it.

"You're an idiot," Edward told himself.

He strode to his bed, dove in, and pulled up the covers. His flashlight had a broad base, so he could set it upright. He did that, then lay back and stared at the distorted circle of light splayed out over his ceiling. The flashlight's beam hit his small ceiling fan and contorted it into a many tentacled cephalopod. That kind of freaked him out, but he wasn't about to turn out the flashlight. Nope. No way.

Edward focused on the outer edges of the light above him. Another gust of wind hit the house with a *whump*, and more rain sprayed his window. Then the rain and wind hushed for just an instant. In that instant, Edward heard tapping . . . clear, distinct tapping. It sounded like a small animal prancing down the hall.

This time, Edward didn't hesitate. He leaped from his bed, grabbed his flashlight, strode to the door, and threw it open. He aimed his flashlight at the floor, sure he was going to light up whatever was approaching his room.

Nothing was in the hallway.

Outside, the storm's decibel level went back up. The opening to the living room brightened as lightning speared the night again. Thunder roared before the living room even had time to return to its gloom. The wind picked up, and it shrieked around the house. It sounded like angry banshees were descending on the house in abject fury.

But even through all that clamor, Edward heard another sound. This time, it was a ticking sound, but not a regular ticking sound like a clock.

Tick . . . tick, tick, tick . . . tick, tick . . . tick, tick, tick, tick, tick.

The last five ticks came very fast. And then . . . nothing but the storm.

Edward felt like he was going to cry. He couldn't remember ever being this scared, well, except for those few seconds before Jack and Faraday—

Edward moaned and turned to run back into his room. He slammed his door behind him, not caring whether it woke up his mom, even secretly hoping it *did* wake her. He wouldn't have admitted it to anyone, but he wanted his mommy . . . badly.

Edward jumped back into his bed, literally, and curled up in a ball under the covers. He held his flashlight to his chest, cradling it like a teddy bear. If only he had a teddy bear . . .

Edward rolled onto his back and concentrated on calming his ratcheting breath. "You're making it all up," he told himself. "It's all in your head."

He needed a distraction from his out-of-control evil fantasy world. He decided to use what had worked for him in the past. He would recite π.

Out loud, Edward began, "Three point one four

one five nine two six five three five eight . . ." His heart rate began to slow. His muscles started to relax.

He stopped reciting, put his thumb on the flashlight switch, and, resolved, turned it off. He kept the flashlight in his hand, but he let his hand fall down by his side. He returned to his nice tranquilizing numbers: "nine seven nine three two three eight four six two six four three three eight three two seven nine five zero two eight eight four one nine seven one six nine three nine three seven five one zero . . ."

His eyes drooped closed. He felt sleep slip in and wrap its comforting arms around him. He let it take him away from—

A *clunk* followed by a *shush* ripped Edward from sleep. He pulled his arm from under the covers and turned on his flashlight. Its glow landed on the end of the bed . . .

And Jack's mud-streaked smiling face.

Edward screamed . . . and screamed.

Continuing to scream, Edward thrashed backward in his bed, his legs kicking out. His covers got caught in his gyrating feet, and the sheet and blanket pulled off the bed and landed in a pile on the floor.

Edward's bedroom door burst open, and his mother ran into the room, her own flashlight bobbing out in front of her.

"Edward?" She was out of breath. "What in the world?"

In a half second, Edward took in his mom's tangled

hair, her pale makeup-less face, her wrinkled nightshirt. Then he looked beyond her, trying to spot the familiar visage that he knew was attached to a robotic cat.

It was no longer at the foot of the bed.

Where did it go? It had to be in here someplace.

He hadn't imagined that face. It had been that horrible manufactured-Jack face, and it had been staring right at him.

But how?

With shaking hands, Edward shined his light around the room.

"Edward?" his mom repeated.

He worked his tongue around his mouth because his mouth was too dry to speak. "Sorry, Mom," he said finally.

She rubbed her eyes. "What happened?"

Edward kept shining his light around the room. He kept looking for even a hint of movement. But he saw nothing that wasn't supposed to be there.

He looked at his mom. "I was sure something was in here."

His mom turned in a circle, aiming her flashlight into every corner of the room. "What was in here?" she asked.

"Um . . . I'm not sure," Edward lied.

"Do I need to check under the bed for monsters?" His mom grinned at him.

Edward tensed. Was it under the . . . ?

His mom bent over and flashed her light under his

bed. "Nope. No monsters. Just some of your junk and more dust bunnies than should be allowed in here."

She straightened and then bent over again and picked up his covers. Setting down her flashlight, she arranged the covers on the bed.

Edward realized he was still crouched by his headboard. He made himself stretch out his legs, and he slid them under the sheet and blanket.

His mom sat on the bed next to him. "It's the storm. It messed with my sleep a little, too."

Edward nodded.

"Come on, let's get you tucked back in," his mom said.

He let her baby him. He could feel himself trembling, and he hoped she didn't notice.

The storm moved on to torment a different town just before dawn. Edward was awake to listen to it withdraw. He was awake all night.

For reasons he didn't understand, he never heard another odd sound after his mom returned to bed. And he hadn't seen Jack's face anymore that night. Where had it gone?

He spent the better part of the night trying to figure out whether he'd imagined the dirty, stiff white face of his friend at the end of his bed. No, that wasn't true. What he'd been doing was trying to convince himself that he hadn't seen it, that it had been some weird trick of the light, a misperception, his brain turning a lump in the covers into the Jack features. But he knew he was deluding himself. He'd seen what he'd seen.

Jack's face had been looking right at him. It wasn't something that looked like anything else. But Edward sure wished it was . . . because after that night, he began seeing the horrid Jack face everywhere.

The first time Edward saw the Jack face again, he was getting off the bus at the end of the day after the storm. Apparently, his classmates had stopped feeling sorry for him, and now they were mad at him for suggesting Schrödinger's cat as a paper topic. Pausing to flick off a spitball that hit him just as he went down the bus's steps, his gaze landed on the yellow mums that surrounded Mrs. Phillips's baseball-cap-wearing gnomes. Her gnomes wore the caps starting in September, until the World Series was over.

Edward was shrugging into his backpack when he saw the face. It was right where he and Jack had found Faraday, and it was peering up at Edward from under a low-hanging rhododendron branch.

Edward gasped and stared. Then he blurted, "What do you want?"

"What do I want?" Mrs. Phillips asked.

Edward jumped and looked up Mrs. Phillips's walkway.

"A magical weed disappearer," Mrs. Phillips said. "Do you have one of those?"

The widow was kneeling at the edge of her walkway

pulling weeds; long gray hair spilled over her hunched shoulders. She wore a bright fuchsia running suit and purple tennis shoes.

"Oh, hi, Mrs. Phillips. I didn't see you there."

She frowned at him, brushing dirty fingers across her tan, lined face. "Then who were you talking to?"

"Huh?" Edward flicked his gaze back down to the flower bed. Jack's face was gone.

He looked again at Mrs. Phillips. "Oh, I was just practicing lines for a school play."

Mrs. Phillips smiled. "Good for you. I wish you luck with that." She returned to her weeding, and Edward waved good-bye and turned to continue down the street.

As he walked, he scanned his surroundings. Where had the Friendly Face gone?

Or more important, had he really seen it again?

Before he'd left for school that morning, Edward had considered going out into the yard to see if the thing was still buried there, but there was no way to do it without his mom knowing about it. She left for work right when he left to catch the bus.

Now he wasn't sure if he wanted to know if the Jack-faced cat was still in the hole. If it was, that meant . . . what? That he was losing his mind? Or that the nasty thing had the ability to dig itself out and rebury itself, just to torment him?

It's all infinite possibility, Jack's voice whispered into his mind. Unfortunately, Edward wasn't a fan of duality right now; it suggested far too many alarming options.

Edward hurried up the sidewalk. In dizzying contrast to yesterday and the previous night, today was mild and sunny. Several people in the neighborhood were out cleaning up debris from the storm. A lot of branches had come down. Leaves and twigs were everywhere. Edward heard at least three leaf blowers and one lawn mower. The air smelled like mulch.

Just before Edward got to his own walkway, he caught a glimpse of something white out of the corner of his eye. Turning, he was sure he saw the Jack-faced cat trot around behind his neighbor's house. Edward stared. Should he go after it?

He felt his legs start to shake. Well, there was his answer. He was too much of a coward to go after the thing and . . . what? Confront it? Destroy it?

He had no idea what to do.

So, he'd do nothing.

Edward ran up his walkway, scrabbled at the lock on his front door, and dashed inside. He slammed the door behind him. Leaning against it, he took several deep breaths.

Should he go in the backyard and dig?

He had to.

Heading to the door before he could change his mind, Edward went out into the backyard and looked at the spot where he'd buried the Jack-faced cat. The mound was flattened down, but the rain could have done that. Given that a small puddle had collected on top of where the mound had been, that was likely.

Other than the puddle, the area looked just the way Edward had left it.

"Edward?"

Edward spun around. His mom stood on the back deck.

"What are you doing?" she called.

"Oh, just checking for, um, storm damage."

"Good thinking. That's why I came home early. Want to help me do a little yard cleanup?"

So much for digging up the hole. Edward couldn't help but notice he felt relieved.

"Sure," he said. He turned his back on the Friendly Face's burial spot and walked toward his mom.

By the time Edward went to bed that evening, he was too tired to even care what the Friendly Face was doing. And the next day, the kids at school were so derisive, he began to think it might be nice to have the Friendly Face around after all. Maybe the freakish robot was the only friend he could hope to have.

But no. He didn't want that thing as a friend. He didn't want it at all.

Which was why, by the end of the week, Edward was a fidgety mass of overreactive nerves. It didn't seem to matter what he wanted. He kept seeing the Jack-faced cat everywhere.

Or at least he thought he did.

When Edward and Jack had been in junior high school, they'd ferreted out all the good secluded spots in the building, places they could hang out without encountering other kids. They'd often talked about how their first task as freshmen would be to find those sorts of places in the high school. Well, Jack wasn't here to help, but Edward still went looking for seclusion, and he found it . . . in an old, unused supply closet; under a back stairway; in a hidden courtyard; behind the teachers' lounge; behind a section of collapsible bleachers in the gym. But everyplace he found, the Jack-faced cat found, too. He only got to use each of his reclusive spots once before he spotted the face peering at him from the deepest shadows of the hidden areas.

Twice, he was sure he saw the Friendly Face hunched under the bushes near the school's entrance, tucked among the leaves, just out of view of the casual passerby. At home, he spotted Jack's face in the bushes and plants in his yard—poking up through the hydrangeas outside the kitchen window, peering past the boxwood hedge outside the living room window, and lurking in the branches of the drooping forsythia bush under his own window.

And the sounds he'd heard the night of the storm . . . now he heard them everywhere. Chittering, ticking, bizarre pneumatic pattering sounds—he heard those all the time now in his hiding places at school, in his house. He'd heard the strange sibilant pitter-patter outside his door every night this week.

Granted, he'd never opened his door to see just what was out there. But he had slept with his lights on. He'd wait until after his mom went to sleep, and he'd turn on his brass lamp. The first night, he didn't sleep well with all that light. The next night, though, he went right to sleep, probably because he was so exhausted from two nights of practically no sleep.

Now it was Friday, four days since the storm, and Edward still hadn't gone out to dig up the Jack-faced cat's "grave." Two days after the storm, it had started raining again, and it hadn't stopped . . . until today.

The sun came out at noon, while Edward ate his peanut butter sandwich by himself next to a window in the school cafeteria. It was then that he decided he had to check the hole when he got home. If the Friendly Face was still there, he might have to ask his mom to take him for an MRI. Maybe he had a tumor. Or maybe he *was* going crazy. Maybe he'd imagined the whole Friendly Face thing, from start to finish. The very concept seemed outlandish to him, even now.

After school, Edward was running late when he trotted toward the bus. He had enough time, but he wouldn't be able to pick his seat the way he wanted to. There were certain kids he never wanted to sit beside, kids who liked to torture him more than others.

He was late because he'd gone into the deserted restroom after his last class. While washing his hands, he'd glanced in the mirror and spotted the Jack face looking over his shoulder at him. But when he'd wheeled around, there was nothing there. He thought he heard a pattering behind a vent cover that looked askew, and he was debating whether he should check it when three other boys had burst into the restroom. Edward had been forced to run before they tried to stick his head in the toilet.

Now Edward was just a few feet from the bus when Eddy, one of the particularly obnoxious guys in his class, deliberately bumped into him. Edward staggered and almost fell. He was close enough to the bus to put out a hand and catch himself. When he did, he got a glimpse of the Jack face peeking out at him from behind the bus's back fender. It was clinging to the emergency exit, hidden between Edward's bus and the bus behind, down low where no one—except Edward—could see it.

It was *on* his bus.

Edward backed away. He was bumped again, this time by Julia.

"Watch where you're going!" she snapped at him.

"Sorry." He didn't even look at her pretty wavy hair as he continued to backpedal.

The buses in front of Edward's started to roll forward.

"Coming?" the bus driver called from inside.

Edward looked at the wheel well where he'd seen the Jack face. He thought he saw movement, but he wasn't sure.

"No. I forgot something. I'll walk. Thanks."

Don shrugged and closed the bus door. The bus pulled out. Edward stared after it but didn't see anything except kids through any of the windows.

After the buses were gone, Edward sighed. He'd just let his paranoia force him into a six-mile walk. *Brilliant.* Sighing again, Edward settled his backpack more comfortably on his shoulders and started walking down the school driveway.

The road that led from the school back into town didn't have any sidewalks, just a narrow gravel verge that was snug up against the massive tree trunks lining the road. Along the verge, ferns and other low-growing underbrush created a green shaggy carpet that extended into the dusky depths of the forest. Here and there, the shaggy carpet gave way to beds of fallen fir needles. These were the paths that a lot of kids used to head into the woods. Not Edward. He would stay out here on the road, thank you very much.

A few cars motored past Edward. One of them honked its horn. He had no idea who was in it.

He coughed on the gas fumes that lingered in the wake of the last car. He turned to look behind him to see if more cars were coming.

He froze. No cars were coming up the road. But something was.

It was the Friendly Face.

It was right there, clear as could be, no mistaking it for anything else. This wasn't one of those fleeting glimpses. This wasn't just a peek of the pale Jack face. This was the honest-to-goodness real Friendly Face, the black cat, its fur now matted and muddy—possibly from being buried and digging itself out—and the haunting Jack features with the unyielding smile. The Jack-faced cat was skipping along the edge of the road, gamboling happily after Edward as if they were playing a game of follow-the-leader.

Edward didn't stop to think. He just ran.

At first, he ran down the road, but when he checked over his shoulder, he could see that Jack's face was getting closer. There was no way he could outrun an animatronic on a flat, open road. He had no choice if he wanted to get way. He veered to his left, in between two towering trees.

Edward scraped his shoulder against the bark of the second tree, but he kept running. He leaped over a scrubby bush, and he trampled a cluster of ferns. He didn't take time to look behind him again. He just fled, pell-mell, through the damp and dingy woods.

A few hundred feet into the trees, Edward reached a creek. He didn't slow down. He splashed across it. He raced up the incline on the other side of the creek, slipping when his feet encountered a pile of river rocks.

Windmilling his arms to get his balance, Edward turned, intending to run along the flat part of the terrain here, instead of having to climb any higher up from the creek. But a splash made him check back behind him again.

The cat thing was capering along in Edward's wake. Its tail was up in the air as if it was having the time of its life. Life? It had no life. It wasn't alive! It was a thing!

Edward wasn't fooled by the thing's happy expression. The smile was too set, too hard to suggest any good feelings. Given that the Jack-faced cat was functioning, moving, maybe even—*God forbid*—thinking, it was fair to say it was alive, at least in a robotic way. That meant when he'd put it in the hole and covered it with dirt, he buried it alive. Was it angry?

What would it do when it reached him?

Edward squeaked in panic and turned to run again. Scrambling up a slippery bank, he fell to his knees, and clawed his way to the top.

Realizing that his backpack was slowing him down, Edward shrugged out of it, and he managed to get back on his feet. His breath came in ragged gasps, and he ordered his legs to keep going, to run, *hard*.

It had been stupid to run into the forest. He'd have been better off on the road, where there were other people, where someone might be able to pull over and help him.

He tried to think it through while he ran, tried to discern whether he was still being followed. At first, all he could hear were his own footfalls and labored breathing. But then he heard the ticking and that pneumatic-sounding patter.

His throat tightened.

Frenzied, he plowed his way through a dense thicket of some greenery he didn't recognize and found the creek again. It had curled around. He figured if he recrossed it, he'd end up back at the road eventually.

Could he stay out in front of the Jack-faced cat long enough to get there?

He risked a glance over his shoulder.

"Go away," he screeched when he saw the thing frisking along merrily, bouncing and hopping playfully in the furrows Edward's feet left in the undergrowth.

He put his back to Jack's face and stumbled toward the creek again. When he reached it, he leaped across its deepest part. His foot landed on a rock, and his ankle twisted. He cried out, but he didn't go down. Tears filled his eyes as he kept running, ignoring the throbbing pain.

He wasn't sure how long he ran after he crossed the creek. It felt like he was running in circles. Was that the same tree he'd just passed? How could he tell? They all looked alike.

He didn't look back again. The occasional *tick-tick-tick* was enough to let him know his pursuer was still after him.

The pain in his ankle got worse every time his foot pounded the ground. His legs started feeling weak. He could hear rales in his lungs. His felt his heart trying to hammer its way out of his chest.

He was beginning to think he was going to run himself into death from exhaustion when he noticed light creeping in between the trees ahead. He thought he heard the rush of an engine going past on the road.

He was almost there.

He tried to run faster, but he was so tired. His steps faltered.

Something touched Edward's ankle. He glanced down. The Jack face smiled up at him.

Edward screamed, put his head down, and pumped his arms to push his body even faster. Just a few more steps. He sprinted hard, his gaze firmly on the ground in front of him so he wouldn't trip over something and go down.

He couldn't see clearly though. Everything was blurry, probably because his eyes were filled with tears and sweat.

It didn't matter. He kept running.

He bolted forward, pelting away from the thing behind him, hurtling toward what he hoped was—

Edward felt a flash of pain so intense that it couldn't possibly have been real. The pain was the last thing he felt. That the pain was incomprehensible was the last thing he thought. He never even had a chance to think, *Sorry.*

The semitruck that hit Edward started skidding right after the impact. The driver, his eyes bulging, his heart racing, his stomach suddenly in a bilious knot, practically stood on the truck's brake pedal. Of course, it was too late. The semitruck kept going for several yards before jackknifing to a stop.

Well behind the truck, Edward's body lay in the road, a pool of blood widening around it. A few feet away, partially hidden in the ferns at the edge of the verge, the Friendly Face hunkered down. It flicked its robotic tail. Its smiling Jack face kept its gaze serenely focused on Edward's still form.

It would wait now. It would wait patiently for Edward to get back up so they could play some more.

Mott lingered at the edge of the arcade in Freddy Fazbear's Pizzeria and contemplated why he still liked this place so much. Was it the decor? The food? The animatronics? No. The truth was that Freddy's—bright, loud, and always over the top—was just a fun place to be. He turned and surveyed the dining area stretching out from the arcade. Even the parents were having a good time. Technically, he should have been outgrowing this place, but Freddy's had a way of getting under the skin.

"Mott?"

Mott looked down at Rory, his spastic little brother.

"Can we get more tickets?" Rory asked. "I almost beat Ben at air hockey. I need a do-over."

Mott reached out to ruffle Rory's bright red hair. Predictably, Rory, who recently turned seven and was "too grown-up" for things like hair ruffling, darted out of Mott's reach and said, "Mott!" in a way that turned one syllable into three.

Mott laughed and pulled a wad of dollar bills from his jeans pocket. "Go beat the pants off him."

Rory grinned, grabbed the money, and took off.

On the stage that ran the length of Freddy's dining room, Freddy Fazbear and his cohorts, Bonnie and Chica, began a new song. A spinning disco ball overhead started spraying streams of yellow, red, green, and purple light all over the pizzeria. Mott tapped his foot and began singing along under his breath.

"Mott!" a girl called out.

He turned to look at the packed tables. A couple of four- and five-year-olds bumped into him as they went racing past. He smiled. Had he run around nonstop like that when he was their age? If he had, he could understand his mom's claim that he was responsible for 90 percent of the wrinkles forming on her still-young face.

"Over here!" the girl called again.

He saw a slender, pink-nailed hand waving from a table a few feet away. It was Theresa, one of the popular girls in his class. He grinned at her, glanced once to check on Rory, and then sauntered across Freddy's black-and-white-checkered floor.

Theresa shared a red-cloth-covered, pizza-and-soda-laden table with a man and a woman who had to be her parents. They all shared the same warm brown, almost amber eyes, although neither parent had Teresa's gorgeous smile. Her parents were turned away from her, talking animatedly with another couple at the next table. Mott heard something about golf and the cost of airfare.

Mott turned his attention to Theresa. Friendly, smart, and petite, Theresa was what his mom called a "catch." Though they shared English and algebra classes, they hadn't talked much outside class. Still, she always smiled at him in the hallways.

"Hey, Theresa."

"Hi, Mott. Are you here alone?" Theresa gestured at the empty chair next to her, and Mott took it.

A ponytailed server on roller skates zipped past with a fresh pizza. Aromas of tomato, basil, and cheese teased Mott's nose. His mouth watered. He hadn't eaten before he and Rory came here, figuring they'd get a pizza right away. But Rory had been obsessed with the games since they'd arrived, and they hadn't ordered anything yet. Mott was getting so hungry that even the sickly sweet blue-frosted birthday cake that sat near the stage was starting to look good.

"No," he said. "I'm here with my little brother. He's friends with the birthday boy."

"Same here—my little brother, too."

"Which one is yours?" Mott asked, mainly because he had no idea what else to say.

Theresa pointed at a boy with dark curls dancing with a bunch of little kids up next to the stage.

"Yours?" she said.

He looked over at the arcade. Rory's bright hair made him easy to spot: He and Ben had left the air hockey table and were charging this way. Rory probably wanted more money for tokens.

"Wow, really? He doesn't look like you," Theresa said.

Mott wasn't sure what to say to that, so he just shrugged. But she was right. Rory got his red hair from their mother. Mott had their dad's plain brown hair, thankfully. Rory, with tufts of red that refused to lie down properly on his head, his overlarge eyes and mouth, and his face full of freckles, was always going to be kind of goofy-looking. Mott, on the other hand, had been getting girls' stares long before he wanted to. When he turned thirteen a few months before, he finally began to welcome all that attention. According to his mom, he was "objectively good-looking." The components of this assessment apparently were his naturally wavy hair, his "hooded" dark brown eyes, his "strong chin," and his "great teeth." In the last couple months, he'd also shot up a few inches, and he'd started working out. His shoulders were getting broad. He was beginning to see what his mom saw. Apparently, girls like Theresa were seeing it, too.

"Don't let it go to your head," his mom had told him. "If you do, I'll ground you for the rest of your life."

Smiling at the memory, he said to Theresa, "On a good day, I'll admit Rory looks like our mom. On a bad day, I tell him he was left on our doorstep by sea monkeys."

Rory raced up to the table just in time to hear what Mott had said. "I was not!" he shouted. Then he stuck out his hand. "I want more tickets!"

Mott sighed and dug in his pocket for a few more dollars. He'd have paid several hundred dollars to make Rory go away so he could keep talking to Theresa.

Rory took the money Mott held out and ran off without saying thank you.

Theresa laughed, then made a face. "I hate sea monkeys."

Mott laughed, too. "*Exactly.* Creepy little things." He winked. "The real ones, not my brother."

Theresa shivered. "I know what you mean. The real ones are like centipedes with tentacles and tails."

Freddy and his band segued into another cover of a popular song, this one with a rocking beat. Theresa scooted her chair closer to Mott. "This is a good song, don't you think?"

Mott nodded. "I do, but I think I like this group's

ballads better." He named another song by the same group who'd originally done this one.

Theresa bounced in her seat. "Oh, yeah, that's a really good one. You like ballads? I'm learning to play the guitar, and that's what I like to sing."

"I'd love to hear you sing sometime," Mott said.

Theresa beamed at him.

They spent the next several minutes talking music, and Mott had pretty much forgotten where he was until he glanced up and saw Rory galloping over, bouncing off a couple other little kids and two tables as he came. He was grinning wildly, and he held up what looked like a new toy . . . something in bright-colored cardboard and plastic packaging.

Rory was going so fast that when he got to the table he plowed right into Mott and started to lose his balance. Mott grabbed his brother's arm and kept him upright.

"Look what I got, Mott!" Rory half yelled, half screamed.

He was only a few inches from Mott now, and Mott winced at the excessive decibel level. As he often did, he wished Rory had a volume control he could dial down.

Rory's blaring announcement had gotten Theresa's and her parents' attention. They all smiled at Rory as Mott asked, with as much enthusiasm as he could muster, "What did you get?"

Rory started waving around his treasure. He waved it so rapidly that Mott still couldn't tell what it was.

He frowned, trying to read the words on the waving package.

"Sea Bonnies!" Rory said. "I got Sea Bonnies! Look!" He kept waving the package.

"I'm trying to look," Mott said. He reached out and snatched the package.

Rory jumped up and down like he was on an invisible pogo stick.

Mott focused on the package in his hand. Against a black-checked background, bright red letters announced that the package contained "Astounding Live Sea Bonnies!" Under the words, the image of a seriously disquieting little purplish-blue creature that appeared to be a cross between a sea monkey and a rabbit was encircled by a bright blue blob of what was probably supposed to be water. Next to the image, the package promised, "Contains everything you need to grow and nurture your own Sea Bonnies." Beneath that, plastic sheathing covered four packets, "Designed to start your own healthy colony of happy Sea Bonnies." There were two packets of "Sea Bonnie LIVE EGGS," one of "Sea Bonnie Water Purification Powder," and one of "Sea Bonnie Super-Duper Growth Food." At the bottom of the packaging, bright blue letters proclaimed, "Guaranteed to live for three years!"

Mott made a face and looked at Rory. "Really?"

Rory was still hopping up and down. Now he giggled and shouted, "You said sea monkeys left me on the doorstep. Not sea monkeys! Sea Bonnies!" Rory let loose with one of his high-pitched laughs. He clearly thought he was hilarious. He spun in a gleeful circle. "Now I can have some of my *real* brothers and sisters around." He laughed some more, quite pleased with himself.

Mott shook his head. He felt Theresa leaning in behind him, and he showed her the package.

"Ew," she said.

He nodded in agreement.

Rory plucked the package from Mott's hand. "They're awesome!"

"Sure they are," Mott said.

As soon as Mott and Rory got home, Rory darted into the kitchen to find their mother, who was tearing up lettuce for a salad. Beef stew simmered on the six-burner Viking range that was his mom's pride and joy. She loved to cook. Rory showed his mom the Sea Bonnies package and started talking nonstop as he climbed up onto one of the wood stools in front of the granite-covered island where she worked.

Their mom set the lettuce aside and began chopping tomatoes and cucumbers for the salad. For one blissful moment, all Mott could hear was the faint hum of the fan above the range, the intermittent tap of his mom's knife against the cutting board, and the delicious stew bubbling. But then Rory started jabbering, and all Mott could hear was his chatterbox of a brother.

Rory waved his Sea Bonnies package under his

mother's nose. She blinked at it but kept working on the salad. Rory didn't seem to care.

"Sea Bonnies are basically like sea monkeys, but they're genically engined to look like Bonnie, you know Bonnie from Freddy's," Rory said.

Mott and his mother exchanged a smile at Rory's version of "genetically engineered."

Rory kept talking. "They're super-cool looking, and Fazbear Entertainment only came out with them last month. That's what Ben said. He usually buys all the new stuff, but his parents wouldn't let him get any Sea Bonnies because they said Puter might eat them, and they didn't think that would be good for Puter, and that wouldn't be good for the Sea Bonnies, either." He giggled wildly.

Mott looked at his mom over the top of Rory's head. He shrugged.

Wearing her usual stay-at-home clothes—black yoga pants and a baggy white shirt—his mom brushed a strand of red hair from her blue eyes. She scratched her freckled nose and smiled.

"Puter is the family cat, right?" his mom said.

"Hm? Oh yeah," Rory said. "Don't you think I should get a bigger fish tank now that Fritz's going to have friends? I mean, I know the small one fits on my desk, and the Sea Bonnies can help Fritz keep me company while I do homework and color and stuff. But if we got me a big tank with a stand, I could put it on the other side of the room, under the window. Oh, no, wait. What if we got a *huge* one, and we put it in the living room? Oh, no, wait. Then I wouldn't have them in my room. I think I want them in my room. Maybe I could get more and we could get two tanks and . . ."

While Rory talked and Mott tried not to listen to him, their mom wiped her hands on a dish towel. She stepped over and gently put a hand over Rory's mouth. "Take a breath, sweetie," she said.

"It's genetically engineered," Mott said in the blessed quiet that suddenly filled the kitchen. "Not genically engined."

His mom gave him a look and shook her head. He rolled his eyes.

She crossed the shiny wood floor to the stainless-steel refrigerator and opened it to grab a bottle of salad dressing. "Do Sea Bonnies have the same water temperature requirement that Fritz has?" she asked.

Rory said, "Huh?"

"May I see the package?" Mott asked Rory.

Rory shrugged and handed it over.

Mott scanned the instructions on the back of the package. He frowned. "Isn't it seventy-four degrees now?"

His mother nodded.

"The water needs to be seventy-five to eighty-one degrees for them to hatch. Then it can go back down. I wonder if cranking it up to, like, seventy-eight or something would be okay for a goldfish for the twenty-four hours it takes to hatch the Sea Bonnie eggs?"

"Maybe you can research that after dinner," his mom said.

Mott shrugged. "Sure. Why not? That's what all the cool kids do on Saturday nights."

She laughed. "No, that's what the cool kids *wish* they were doing. Instead, they're going to boring things like movies and parties."

"I feel sorry for them," Mott said.

Rory, who had been examining his Sea Bonnies with great pride and joy, suddenly pointed at a spot on the package. "What's that word?"

Mott looked under his brother's dirty index finger. "Colony."

"What's a colony?"

Mott let his mom take that one. When she finished defining the word, Rory screwed up his face and announced, "I want an *empire*, not a colony. That's bigger, right? Maybe I should get another package of them."

"One package is enough," his mom told him.

Rory squinted and took a deep breath, in clear preparation for a loud rebellion.

Mott spoke quickly. "You can call it whatever you want, you know."

Rory tilted his head. "I can?"

"Absolutely," Mott and his mom said in unison.

After dinner and after determining that Fritz wouldn't be harmed by a day or so of seventy-eight-degree water, Mott helped Rory get his tank set up for the Sea Bonnies.

Rory's tank was small, maybe sixteen inches by ten inches or so. It held five gallons . . . more water than Fritz needed, but Mott thought Fritz always looked content in his domain. Mott idly wondered what Fritz would think about the soon-to-be interlopers. Did fish think?

Lifting the tank's lid and waiting while Rory said hello to Fritz, Mott opened the Sea Bonnie packaging.

"Okay, the first step," he told Rory, "is to put this in." He handed Rory the packet of water purifier. At Rory's insistence, he read the ingredients: salt, some kind of water conditioner, and some brine shrimp eggs.

"That's all we can do today," Mott told a frustrated Rory when his little brother wanted to dump all the other packets in, too.

"The instructions say to wait twenty-four hours. Then we'll put in the eggs. Those will be the genetically engineered eggs."

"Why do we have to wait?" Rory scowled.

Mott shrugged. "Because the packaging says so." He didn't bother telling Rory that the whole process was weird. He read the contents of the eggs packet, and he was surprised to see it also contained yeast, borax, soda, salt, and blue dye.

"What about this?" Rory asked, holding up the food packet.

Mott referred to the instructions. "That goes in after the eggs hatch."

The food packet contained more yeast and some spirulina. It would have to be added every few days.

Because Mott didn't trust Rory not to dump everything in the tank at once, he took the packets when he left Rory's room. Rory protested, but when he started to throw a tantrum, their mom appeared to smooth things over.

Mott felt bad that she had to intervene. Their dad was a commercial airline pilot who was often away, which meant Mom had to run the house and do most everything at home. She also worked full-time at an event-planning firm and was trying to start her own company in her spare time (of which she had little). To compound matters, most of the events she planned happened in the evening, and she had to be there to oversee them. Mott wasn't sure when his mom slept. And even with all that, she never acted annoyed when she was interrupted.

"Mom," Mott said, "I'll get him ready for bed. Go rest."

"Sure?" she asked.

"Sure."

"You're a good son," his mom said.

"I know." He laughed.

With just a little wheedling, Mott got Rory into the bathroom to brush his teeth. While he brushed, Rory chattered about school and his friends and the new puppy that Danny and his family had gotten a couple weeks before. Toothpaste shot all over the place as Rory talked.

Used to this routine, Mott wiped down the counter and the floor. Eventually, Rory spit the remainder of his toothpaste into the sink. Mott used a wet washcloth to wipe Rory's face. Rory wriggled out of his reach.

"I want a puppy," Rory said. "When's Dad coming home?"

"He's doing nonstops this week," Mott said. He'd opted for answering the second question first. It was easier. "I think he'll be home for a few days next week."

"Maybe he'll get us a puppy while he's home," Rory said.

"Maybe Mom will get us a puppy when you demonstrate a little responsibility."

Rory twisted his lips in concentration. "How do I do that?"

Mott considered what he could get away with. "Well, maybe if you cleaned up your room, didn't yell so much, and stopped interrupting me and Mom whenever—"

Rory shouted, "No! I know what I can do!"

"Shh."

Rory lowered his voice, to just above normal volume. "I can help Danny with Dapup."

"Dapup?" Mott repeated.

"That's the puppy's name. His dad kept asking, 'Where's da puppy?' and his mom said they might as well call him that. His whole name is Dapuppy, but they call him Dapup. Danny likes to follow Dapup

around and say over and over, 'What's up, Dapup?'"
Rory giggled gleefully.

Mott laughed. He couldn't help it. Rory was a lot of
annoying things, but he was also entertaining as all get
out. Apparently, so were Danny and his family.

"Okay," Mott said. "Let's get you to bed."

Following Rory into his room, Mott shut Rory's
bedroom door so Rory's jibber-jabber didn't bother
their mother.

"Now Danny's bugging his parents for a kitten," Rory
went on. "He wants to name it Dacat or Dakitten."
Rory launched himself toward his bed, spun in midair,
and landed on his back. He kicked his legs in the air
like an upturned beetle and let out another trill of
giggles.

"Where are your pj's, goofus?" Mott asked.

Rory sat up, his eyes dancing. He grabbed his pillow.
"Under the bed, doofus!"

Mott bent over to look under the bed, and a pillow
hit him in the side of the head. He rose to find Rory
looking at the ceiling and whistling.

Mott glanced around as if searching for something.
"Hm. A pillow just hit me in the head. I wonder where
it came from."

Rory giggled.

"Did it come from under the bed?" Mott asked. He
stuck his head under the bed and spotted green-and-
yellow dinosaur-patterned pj's. As he reached for them,
another pillow struck his shoulders.

Mott whipped his head out from under the bed and jumped to his feet, feigning shock and outrage. He dropped the pj's on the bed. "Another one? Is there an invisible Pillow Thrower in the room?" He whirled in a circle, wearing a fierce expression as Rory giggled louder.

"Show yourself, you pillow-throwing milksop!" Mott leaned over and picked up the thrown pillows. "I'll beat you in a fair fight, if you have the mettle!" He struck a warrior pose, both pillows raised.

Rory, struggling against a rising tide of giggles, shouted, "What's a milksop, and why does he need metal?"

Mott cocked his head. "Hark, methinks these questions are a misdirect." He glowered at Rory. "Dost thou do the Pillow Thrower's bidding, young lad? Are thee in cahoots with the namby-pamby?"

Rory laughed so hard he snorted. He reached for the only remaining pillow on the bed. Mott turned his back to Rory and pretended to look for the Pillow Thrower again. The third pillow hit him in the back.

"Outrageous!" he bellowed, leaning to pick up the latest pillow. He rotated to face Rory. "I've no choice but to unleash my retaliation upon thine own countenance, young minion of the invisible Pillow Thrower!" Making sure he didn't throw too hard, Mott fired all three pillows at Rory, who dove under the covers squealing and laughing.

Mott fell on him and started tickling him. Rory shrieked and laughed louder.

"Dost thou surrender?" Mott asked.

Rory gasped. "Yes! Yes!" His breath smelled like his peppermint toothpaste.

Mott stopped tickling his brother. Rory, his face flushed, his eyes wet with happy tears, grinned up at Mott. "You didn't answer my question."

Mott reached for the pj's, which had landed on the floor again during the roughhousing. "What . . . ? Oh, you mean *milksop* and *mettle*?"

Rory nodded.

Mott handed Rory his pj's. "Put these on. A milksop is someone who is indecisive or doesn't have courage. It comes from how little kids used to sop up milk with their bread."

Rory frowned, then nodded. "I like that word."

"And it's *m-e-t-t-l-e*, not *m-e-t-a-l*," Mott said as Rory pulled on his pj top. "*Mettle*," he spelled it again, "means the ability to cope with difficulties, someone who can bounce back from an attack easily."

Rory exchanged his jeans for his pj pants. "That's another good word."

"I agree," Mott said. "Let's get you under the covers."

Rory yawned and crawled under the covers, headfirst.

Mott rolled his eyes. "Turn around, goofus."

Rory giggled from under the covers. He rotated and his tousled head appeared. "What's *namby-pamby*?"

Mott helped Rory get situated in bed. "It's another

word for milksop, but it also means someone without much strength."

"I'm not a namby-pamby or a milksop," Rory said.

"No, you aren't," Mott agreed.

Mott got home late on Monday evening. He and his two best friends, Nate and Lyle, had to work on a science project, and they'd met at Nate's house to work on it. Nate's dad, Dr. Tabor, aka Dr. T, was a pediatrician who had been Mott's doctor since Mott was a baby. Nate and Mott had become friends because they'd met at Dr. Tabor's office when they were about two. Dr. T's wife, an engineer, had an important meeting that day, so Dr. T had brought his son to work with him. Nate and Mott had taken over the blocks in the waiting room play area, building an impressive fort that none of the other kids in the waiting room were allowed to touch. Dr. T had told Mott's mom that the boys' friendship clearly was meant to be and suggested the parents get together for dinner while the kids had a playdate. Or at least, that's what Mott's mom had told him. He didn't remember any of it. All he knew was that his parents were good friends with Nate's parents, and he was good friends with Nate.

His earliest memory of Nate was the two of them trying to climb up on a counter to steal freshly baked cookies. They'd both ended up in Dr. T's office with contusions and mild burns from the hot cookie sheets. Not that Mott remembered that, either. He just remembered the chair ladder they'd built, and he remembered a lot of pain.

Over the years, Dr. T had become like a dad to Mott. Dr. T believed that work and home life should be properly balanced, so he opened his clinic near the neighborhood, close to the end of the greenbelt that ran past the back of Mott's house. Dr. T started work really early, but he never worked late, never worked weekends, and he was always ready and willing to play or help with school.

Tonight, he was helping the boys get started on their science project, which was a study of the effects of antibiotics on microorganisms. Having access to a doctor came in handy. Dr. T had gotten a small amount of four types of antibiotics (penicillin, streptomycin, Aureomycin, and Terramycin). He'd also gotten a syringe, a petri dish, flasks and beakers, and some pipettes. Mott and his friends had been tasked with getting everything else they'd need: a potato, agar, dextrose, distilled water, garden soil, and pens that would write on glass. When they'd complained about the agar and dextrose—"What in the heck are those?" Nate had asked his dad—Dr. T had gotten them, too.

Dr. T and Nate had already done 99 percent of the experiment. Lyle was bored out of his mind and mostly tried to make music with the pipettes and the beakers. Mott wasn't bored, but he was puzzled by the complex process, what with this being heated and that being mixed in. Thanks to Dr. T, he did eventually understand what they were doing, and he was looking forward to seeing what microorganism colonies grew in the petri dishes they set next to the heat register in Nate's house. They had bets going on which antibiotics would keep the colonies from growing.

"Two cheeseburgers and a milkshake on penicillin," Nate said.

"I'll take that bet," Lyle said, "if we throw in a couple large fries. How about you, Mott?"

"I'm with Nate," Mott said.

Lyle rolled his eyes. "Well, then if you're wrong, it had better be two milkshakes."

"You're going down," Nate said.

Mott laughed with his friends and said good night. He biked home a little after nine, when it was dark.

When he pulled his bike into the garage, Rory met him at the door leading into the kitchen, flailing around in excitement. "Come look! Come look!"

Mott followed his exuberant brother up the stairs and down the long hallway, pausing only to drop his backpack in his own room. When they went into Rory's room, he pointed and stomped back and forth in front of his desk, as if performing a ceremonial dance on the strewn clothes and toys all over his blue-shag-rug-covered floor. "Look!" he shouted.

Mott stepped over a plastic cement truck, a cardboard castle, and two spaceship models to stand before Rory's fish tank, which sat on Rory's desk, surrounded by a clutter of schoolbooks, coloring books, puzzles, and crayons. Even partially hidden by all the piles, it was clear that the tank no longer contained just water and Fritz. It was now filled with tiny wriggling shapes.

Mott leaned over to get a better look. He immediately wished he hadn't. Straightening, Mott rubbed away the goose bumps that had just erupted all over his forearms.

Oh, this is just wrong.

"Aren't they great?" Rory asked.

Mott rolled his eyes. "You're a seriously weird little kid. What are you? Part sea monster? Are you part"—he gulped loudly—"creep from the deep beyond?"

Rory stopped stomping in glee and turned to frown at Mott. "What do you mean by that?"

Although he'd leaned away from the tank, Mott hadn't been able to pull his gaze from the disgusting things swimming around the goldfish in the tank. The Sea Bonnies had hatched, dozens of them . . . no, make that *hundreds*. They looked like semitranslucent, fleshy pale bluish-purple rabbits with tiny black eyes and almost microscopic furry tentacles lining their bodies. From what Mott could tell, they appeared to propel themselves through the water using their misshapen rabbit ears.

Rory tugged on the hem of Mott's brown polo shirt.

"Huh?" Mott said.

"Why did you say that? Why'd you say I'm part sea monster?" Rory punched Mott's leg hard enough to make Mott grimace. "That was mean!"

Ignoring his brother's upset, Mott pointed to the Sea Bonnies. "You actually like these things?" he asked.

Rory turned to look at them. His hurt feelings forgotten, he grinned. "Sure! They're super coolio!"

Mott crossed his arms. "Rory, they're disgusting."

"They are not!" Rory kicked out at Mott and barely missed Mott's shin. "That's not nice to say stuff like that. You're going to make them feel bad." He reached out to the fish tank and stroked the glass like he was trying to soothe his mutant pets.

"Whatever," Mott scoffed. He started to turn away and leave the room, but an abrupt movement in the tank yanked his gaze back to the Sea Bonnies.

He lifted his eyebrows.

The Sea Bonnies had moved, in a giant cluster, to where Rory's hand had brushed against the side of the tank. Fritz still swam lazily at the far side of the tank, but the Sea Bonnies were all together near the glass under Rory's hand. It was like they were responding to his gesture.

The goose bumps reappeared on Mott's arms. He shook his head, annoyed with himself for being unnerved by tiny deviant brine shrimp. Their movement must have been some kind of reflexive response to motion or shadow, he figured. He turned toward the door to Rory's room.

"Apologize!" Rory said.

Mott stopped and gave Rory a look. "To you or your swimming freaks there?"

Rory put both his fists on his skinny hips. "Both!"

Mott laughed at his brother.

A burbling sound came from the fish tank, and Mott's attention returned to it. He blinked and stared.

Although Fritz still floated toward the back of the tank, the Sea Bonnies had shifted so they were lined up, in a disturbingly ordered formation, along the front of the fish tank. He couldn't tell for sure because they were so small, but from where he stood, it looked to Mott like all the Sea Bonnies were facing forward . . . looking at him.

Mott swallowed hard and took a step back.

Obviously, the Sea Bonnies weren't in any sort of formation, and they weren't looking at him. That wasn't possible.

"Mott, say you're sorry!" Rory yelled.

"What's going on in here?"

Mott turned to see his mom standing in the doorway of Rory's room. She had a blue laundry basket full of folded clothes propped against her waist.

Rory charged over to her and threw his bony arms around her thighs. He spewed out his grievance so fast that all his words bunched up together: "Mott-called-me-a-sea-monster-and-he-insulted-my-Sea-Bonnies-he-said-they-were-disgusting-he-was-mean-he-won't-apologize."

Mott's mom used her free hand to pat Rory's shoulder. She looked at Mott over the top of Rory's head and raised one eyebrow. Mott knew that look. It said,

You're not wrong, but can you humor your little brother?

He sighed and nodded. "Rory?"

Rory sniffed and turned to frown at Mott.

Mott squatted to look Rory in the eye. "I'm very sorry I insulted you and your friends. I was just kidding, but I shouldn't have kidded you that way."

He noticed that Rory had a smudge of chocolate at the corner of his pouty lips and several blond crumbs on the front of his green-and-blue-striped shirt. His breath smelled like the chocolate chip cookie he'd clearly snuck from the kitchen.

Mott reached out and cleaned up both crumbs and chocolate with his thumb. Rory squirmed away and said, begrudgingly, "It's okay."

Mott glanced at the Sea Bonnies. He realized that he was checking them because he wanted to see if his apology had mollified them any more than it had his brother.

They were swimming around in the tank exactly as you'd expect sea monkey–like creatures to do. He must have imagined their earlier behavior.

But why would he have done that? Was he that freaked out by the abnormal little creatures?

He rotated back to his mother. "Can I help with any of that?" He waved a hand at the laundry basket.

She flashed him a smile. "I've got it. Go ahead. I assume you only worked on science at Nate's, right?"

Mott nodded. She was right. He still had more homework to do.

Mott started to leave the room, but he hesitated when he heard his name being whispered. He looked back at his mom, who was tucking socks into one of the drawers in Rory's dresser.

"Did you say something?" he asked her.

She looked over at him. "Nope."

He stepped into the hallway . . . and he heard it again.

A whisper, *Mott*.

And more. This time, he also heard, *Scaredy-cat*.

He whirled and glared at Rory. "What did you just call me?"

Both Rory and their mom widened their eyes at Mott. "What in the world, Mott?"

He frowned. "Rory didn't just—"

"I'm not doing nothing wrong," Rory said.

"Anything wrong," his mom said automatically. To Mott, she said, "What did you think you heard?"

He shook his head. He had to have been imagining things.

Suddenly, he realized that the whisper he'd heard hadn't been either his mother's or his brother's voice. And come to think of it, the whisper hadn't been a single whisper. It had sounded like several whisper tones coming in unison—mostly together but just slightly off, resulting in a faint echo.

It couldn't be. He glanced at the fish tank.

The Sea Bonnies were swimming around aimlessly, until he looked. Then they suddenly swam to the end of the tank, as a unit. They all looked through the glass at him.

He opened his mouth to ask his mom if she was seeing what he was seeing, and he immediately realized what a bad idea that was.

Pull it together. Their brains aren't large enough to understand complex speech, let alone generate it.

Instead, he returned to his room; clearly he needed some sleep. After closing his door, Mott stared at the knob for an uncomfortable moment. He locked it.

The next morning, Rory was in a dither because he couldn't find his lucky striped socks, which he had to wear because he and his best friend, Danny, were going to have a "swing-off" during recess.

"And this is more important than me preparing for my algebra quiz?" Mott muttered as he pawed through Rory's drawers in frustration. *Not to mention getting to talk to Theresa before class*, he thought.

He heard a whispered response to his internal dialogue: *As if a girl would pay attention to you.*

Mott whipped his head toward Rory, but Rory wasn't even in the room. Mott was in here alone.

Or not.

He turned toward the fish tank.

Sure enough, the Sea Bonnies were all clustered at the end nearest to Mott. They were watching him again.

Before he knew what he was doing, he spat back, "You're just glorified fish bait."

Rory ran into the room. "What'd you say?" He held up one of his striped socks. "This was in the hamper. I don't know where the other one is, though."

Ungluing his eyes from the fish tank, Mott noticed his heart rate had picked up. He swallowed and said, very slowly and very calmly, "Why don't you go check Mom's room? Maybe your socks got mixed up with hers by mistake. When I'm done looking in here, I'll check my socks."

"Okay!" Rory scampered out of the room.

Mott looked at the Sea Bonnies . . . and he flinched.

The water in the fish tank was choppy. He could hear it sloshing, and he could see bubbles shooting up through the middle of the tank. The Sea Bonnies were agitating, as a group, as if . . . as if they were . . .

Mott strode out of Rory's room . . . and he ran right into Rory.

"Oof," Rory grunted loudly. He bounced off Mott and grinned. "Look!" He held up a pair of striped socks, not his own, but similar in color. "Mom's letting me wear her lucky socks. She says they're even luckier than mine."

Mott tried to talk but couldn't. He was too busy processing what he'd just seen.

Rory didn't seem to notice. He went around Mott and dropped to the floor to put on his mother's socks.

Mott's head was suddenly throbbing. He rubbed his temple.

Could simple organisms like Sea Bonnies even get angry?

Because that was what it had looked like in Rory's tank. It had looked like the Sea Bonnies were reacting to his insult.

And before that, it had sounded like they'd been taunting him again.

"Mott?"

Mott blinked and saw his mother standing just outside his parents' room. She wore a beige suit, and her long red hair was in a French braid.

"Why are you standing in the hall?" she asked. "Are you all right?"

Mott frowned. He opened his mouth, but he still couldn't talk. His mouth was horribly dry.

His mom put her hand against his forehead. "You feel warm. Are you coming down with something? Do you want to stay home from school?"

"No!"

Ah, there was his voice.

His mom raised her eyebrows. "Okay, okay. Wow. I must have the weirdest teen in recorded history. I give him a chance to skip school, and he jumps down my throat."

Mott coughed and moistened his teeth with his tongue. "Sorry, Mom. I didn't mean to snap at you. It's just that—"

His mom's phone rang, and she raised a finger.

Thankful for the reprieve, Mott went into his room to get his backpack. Rory thundered in behind him.

"I'm going to take Danny down," he announced. He flexed nonexistent muscles and puffed his cheeks.

Mott turned Rory around and gave him a gentle push out into the hallway. His mom got off the phone and looked at her sons. "Are we ready?"

"Let's get out of here," Mott said. He winced at his mom's strange look. "I mean, let's go."

Mott was in no hurry to get home that afternoon, but he couldn't come up with a decent excuse to be late. His mom had asked him to bike over to the grade school and escort Rory home. And she'd asked him to look after Rory until she got home later that evening. He'd promised he would do that. If he broke his promise, it would mess up her work.

Mott had hoped that when he got home, he could get Rory to play outside, but rain started coming down on their way home, and it was steady by the time they put their bikes away.

"Go get dried off," Mott said to Rory. "Then come to my room, and I'll help you with your homework."

"No. *You* come to *my* room," Rory said. "I'm s'posed to write a poem about something I have that I like a lot. I'm gonna write about my Sea Bonnies. You have to help me."

"Oh, joy," Mott said.

Mott was a little unnerved to notice that his hands were shaking when he left his backpack in his room. Really? He was afraid of tiny squirming sea critters confined to a glorified fishbowl?

"Get a grip," he breathed as he went down the hall into Rory's room.

Rory sat at his desk, a piece of paper in front of him, a pencil grasped tightly in his right hand. He was staring raptly at his Sea Bonnies. Mott eyed the tank warily.

For a few seconds after his gaze landed on the Sea Bonnies, they swam around normally. Then, as if they realized he was in the room, they suddenly shot to the end of the tank and lined up in formation. Hundreds of pinhead-sized black eyes appeared to be focused directly on him.

"Rory!"

"What?" Rory's gaze didn't leave the tank.

"Do you see what they're doing?" Mott asked.

"Huh?" Rory looked over at Mott.

"The Sea Bonnies. See how they're all lined up?"

Rory looked at the Sea Bonnies. They were milling about separately. Mott felt a growl-like sound rise up in his throat. The little monsters! They were messing with him!

You're so easy to mess with, a chorus of whispers tickled his ears.

Mott clamped his hands over his ears and started humming.

He wasn't sure how long he stood there humming.

Probably not long. Rory was capable of sitting still for only a nanosecond or so. He couldn't have been waiting at his desk for long before he started yanking on Mott's shirt.

Mott opened his eyes and looked at his brother. "What, Rory?"

"What's a word that rhymes with *love*?"

"Above, dove." Mott chewed the inside of his cheek. "That's all I can think of right now."

"Above works."

Stupid, the whispers came again.

"I need to go to the bathroom," Mott told Rory. "Stay in here and behave. When you're done with your poem, come and get me in my room."

"But—" Rory began.

Mott didn't wait. He bolted down the hall and escaped into the bathroom.

He wasn't sure how long he remained in the small white-tiled room. He didn't need to use the toilet, so he sat on the edge of the tub and stared at the fish-patterned blue-and-white wallpaper. He shivered.

Was it fish in general that were weirding him out now? He gazed at the wallpaper. Would the blue fish whisper at him, too?

He waited. Nope. No whispers.

That was because the sounds weren't in his head, or at least, they weren't being manufactured in his head. The sounds were coming from the Sea Bonnies. He was sure of it.

"Mott?" Rory shouted through the door. He pounded on the door so hard it rattled in its frame. "I'm ready!"

Mott sighed and stood. Taking a deep breath, he opened the door.

"Come look," Rory said. He motioned for Mott to follow him back to his bedroom.

"I said you can read it in my room," Mott said.

Rory turned and shook his head. "No! You have to come see this. It's super-duper coolio."

Mott swallowed and accompanied Rory.

In Rory's room, Rory walked over to the fish tank and began reading. "When I saw my Sea Bonnies, I felt love. It was like a gift from Freddy above. They're super cool, and they make me glad. I like that 'cause I hate being sad." Rory pointed to the Sea Bonnies and looked over at Mott with a face shining with happiness. "See?" he said. "They like it!"

Mott made himself look in the tank.

Oh, man.

As much as the Sea Bonnies seemed to dislike Mott, they appeared to love Rory. They were all in formation again, lined up at the glass in front of Mott's little brother. Their little see-through tails were shimmying in unison.

Well, at least the revolting little monsters are nice to my brother, Mott thought.

"It's a good poem," Mott said to Rory.

Rory turned to beam at him.

Behind Rory, the Sea Bonnies darted, as one, to the

end of the aquarium, and they all focused on Mott . . . or again, it looked like they did.

"Do you want to go play my video game with me?" Mott asked Rory.

"Really? Sure!" Rory ran toward Mott, his Sea Bonnies and his poem momentarily forgotten.

Mott hummed as he and Rory trotted toward the stairs. Behind him, whispers reached for his ears, but he hummed louder and refused to listen.

Mott managed to avoid his brother's room for the rest of the evening. When his mother got home, he told her Rory had been restless, so Mott hadn't had time to do his homework. She took over Rory duty, and Mott retreated to his room.

Because, distressingly, he could still hear the faintest of whispers in his own room, he put in his earbuds and listened to music while he studied. He kept in the earbuds while he got ready for bed, taking them out only for a couple of minutes to say good night to his mom. Then he went to bed wearing the earbuds. When he got up the next morning, he went from earbuds to shower to earbuds to out the door. He avoided breakfast by telling his mom he had to get to school early to meet with Nate and Lyle so they could talk about an upcoming history project. The truth was their history project was weeks away, but he figured a lie in the interest of remaining sane was a lie worth telling.

Over lunch, sitting with his friends, eating his cheese

sandwich, he thought about telling them what was going on, but he knew his friends. They didn't share more than one serious bone between them. Mostly, they were one big laugh fest. There was no way they'd do anything but make fun of Mott if he told them what he thought about the Sea Bonnies.

After algebra that afternoon, he briefly considered telling Theresa about his experience with the Sea Bonnies. He knew she was as grossed out by them as he was, so she might be inclined to believe him. But . . .

"Maybe next weekend?" she asked him.

Mott realized he'd missed all of whatever she'd just told him. "I'm so sorry," he said. "My head was some-place else."

Theresa laughed. "I do that all the time. I said we're going camping this weekend, but I was wondering if you'd like to get together next weekend and study? I'm having trouble with two-variable linear equations. You seem to be getting it. I was hoping you could help me?"

She looked really pretty today. Her shiny hair was caught back in a yellow scarf that matched her short dress.

Mott grinned. "Sure!" He'd help her shovel manure if she asked.

He didn't think telling a pretty girl that you think tiny mutant brine shrimp were whispering to you was a good way to impress her. He kept his fears to himself.

If only he could stay away from home . . .

But he couldn't. His mom was used to him enjoying being at home. He spent most of his afternoons with Rory and most of his evenings with his mom, when she wasn't at an event. She would find it bizarre if he suddenly wanted to stay over with Nate or Lyle, and his friends would, too. He'd just have to avoid Rory's room.

This plan worked for much of the evening. He got Rory involved in another video game in the living room. Then he suggested they all play a board game after dinner.

When the game concluded, Mott started to tell his mom he had a headache. Unfortunately, she beat him to it.

"Can you get Rory ready for bed, Mott?" His mom held a palm to the side of her head. "I have a tension headache, and I need to lie down."

Mott's reluctance must have shown on his face. She frowned when she looked at him and said, "I'll give you extra allowance this week."

Mott shook his head. "Forget that. It's okay. Sorry. I was just . . . never mind. Of course, I'll get him into bed."

"Let's read *Foxy and Bonnie on the High Seas*," Rory shouted.

Mott's mom drew away from the sound and headed out of the room.

"Dial it down, buddy," Mott said. "Mom has a headache."

"Oh." Rory turned to watch their mom go up the stairs. "Sorry, Mom!" he yelled.

Mott shook his head and ruffled Rory's hair. Rory emitted his multisyllabic "Mott" and galloped up the stairs. Mott turned off all the lights, checked that the doors were locked and the security system was on, and then he followed his brother up to the second floor.

A long twenty minutes later, Mott had Rory settled and in bed. "You need to get to sleep," Mott told his brother. He handed Rory the plush Freddy Fazbear he liked to sleep with.

"Nope," Rory said. "Read." He clutched Freddy and pointed to his nightstand. The book he'd referred to earlier was lying under a rolled-up comic book, a slingshot, and a half-empty package of gum.

Yeah, read, the whispers commanded.

Mott ground his teeth, but he reached for the book.

He knew better than to try to leave Rory's room without reading to him. Rory was quite capable of pitching an ear splitting fit, and if he did that, it would delay Mott's exit from the room even longer. So, he reached for the book and pulled it out, sending the slingshot and the gum to the floor. He didn't bother to pick them up. He just started reading where he'd last left off.

He read fast and he read loudly, but Rory didn't seem to care. He listened raptly for several minutes, and then his eyes began to droop. Mott kept reading loudly; he was almost shouting. Just as he had been with all his silly antics earlier, he was trying to drown out the whispers.

Thankfully, Rory could sleep through a hurricane. He burrowed down under the covers, tucked Freddy under his chin, and closed his eyes tightly. In seconds, Mott could hear Rory's little-kid snores, even over the shouted reading.

Mott stopped reading, laid the book on the nightstand, and stood all in one motion. He was ready to get out of here.

He turned off the wagon-wheel lamp on the nightstand, but the room didn't go dark. Rory had a night-light plugged in near his door, and the fish tank had a light, which was still on.

Mott turned and prepared to sprint out of the room.

Namby-pamby, the whispers taunted.

Mott froze. Feeling like he couldn't back down from a challenge made by something as small as a Sea Bonnie, he turned to glare at the hideous things.

Expecting to see them glaring back at him, he was surprised to find them all clustered together near the back of the tank. He started to walk by, but then he did a double take. They weren't just clustered together. They were clustered together around Fritz. They were attacking him!

Mott made a beeline for the fish tank to save Fritz, but he realized there was nothing he could do without a net. He looked around wildly. Where was the net that he used to remove Fritz when he had to clean the fish tank?

Mott started opening Rory's desk drawers, and then he snapped his fingers. Rory had taken the thing into the bathroom; he had been playing with it in the tub.

Mott tore out of Rory's room. He raced down the hall to the bathroom. Yep. There was the net, sitting on the side of the tub. Grabbing it, Mott ran back into Rory's room. He charged over to the fish tank.

As Mott reached for the tank's lid, he froze. The Sea Bonnies were nowhere near Fritz. They were swimming around in the tank, acting like . . . well, acting like normal Sea Bonnies. And Fritz was swimming around by himself. He looked just fine.

Had Mott imagined what he'd seen?

Mott leaned closer to be sure Fritz was okay. He appeared to be—

Mott blinked and frowned.

Fritz was not okay.

Fritz was different. He didn't appear to be orange anymore. What had the Sea Bonnies done to him?

Ignoring his distaste for the Sea Bonnies, Mott went over to the tank to get a closer look at the goldfish.

Up close, it was clear that not only was Fritz's color off, his shape was weird, too. Now a faded blue, not unlike the color of the Sea Bonnies, Fritz was a little lumpy, as if he'd—

No, hang on. He wasn't lumpy. Mott gasped, but he couldn't pull himself away from the tank. He had to see.

He leaned closer, putting his face almost up to the glass.

Fritz was drifting lazily through a cluster of Sea Bonnies toward the back of the tank. Mott had to wait until Fritz turned to circle toward the front of the tank. He remained still, almost holding his breath, as the no-longer-gold fish came his way.

As soon as Fritz swam toward the front wall of the tank, Mott's stomach turned. He covered his mouth as he stared at the fish.

Mott had been right when he'd first seen it. Fritz wasn't just lumpy. Something was moving inside Fritz. No. Not inside. Mott squinted at the fish as it swam past his gaze.

Something was moving on the outside, too. All of Fritz was in motion, as if—

"Oh gross!" Mott backed away from the tank, but he couldn't stop looking at Fritz.

Not that Fritz was Fritz anymore.

Fritz was no longer a goldfish. He no longer had fish scales and fins. No. Fritz was now a mass of squirming Sea Bonnies. All Fritz's own parts had been replaced with the tiny gelatinous deformed aquatic rabbits.

Mott stared in disbelief and total disgust. As he gaped, he saw a couple of Fritz's scales drifting toward the bottom of the tank. They slowly floated downward until they settled on the rocks. Mott stared at the tiny scales. They were all that was left of the original Fritz.

Mott felt like he was going to be sick.

Fritz swam behind a cluster of Sea Bonnies, and Mott swallowed bile. He made a face and started to turn toward the door, but movement in the tank caught his attention. He glanced back.

All the Sea Bonnies were lined up against the glass, staring at him.

Mott ran from Rory's room.

Mott spent most of the night and the better part of the next day thinking about Fritz . . . or actually, Not Fritz. All this thinking time wasn't technically needed because he'd reached a conclusion about the body-snatched fish within an hour of leaving Rory's room. Lying on his back on his bed, he'd forced himself to think about what he'd seen. After analyzing it from every angle he could think of, he'd decided what he'd seen was not some new version of Fritz, formed out of Sea Bonnies. It was, instead, a Fritz imposter; it was a mass of Sea Bonnies formed to look like Fritz. Why? Because the Sea Bonnies had consumed Fritz, then used what they'd ingested to multiply themselves and take Fritz's place. Mott had decided they were kind of like flesh-eating nanobots, which then took on the form of the thing they'd eaten.

The day after Mott saw Not Fritz for the first time, the day was bright and relentlessly sunny. The weather was all wrong for his mood. He thought a stormy day would have better suited his dark thoughts.

But no matter. His thoughts weren't distracted by

the sunshine. By the time Mott got home from school, he'd reached a conclusion: The Sea Bonnies had to go.

Unfortunately, he came to this conclusion too late in the day. If he'd worked this out earlier, he could have cut school to come home and flush the nasty things. But now Rory was home, and Mott was going to have to figure out a way to get Rory out of his room—no, out of the *house*—so Mott could dispose of the Sea Bonnies.

Rory now sat at the kitchen counter eating his after-school snack of crackers, cheese, and orange juice. Mott leaned against the counter by the sink and watched his brother shower crumbs all over his blue shirt and the floor.

"How about we go outside and toss the ball around?" Mott said. "It's a nice day; everyone should be outside."

"Okay!" Rory shouted. "I'll go get my mitt." Shoving his last two crackers into his mouth and trailing crumbs behind him, he scurried out of the kitchen.

Once they were outside, Mott started working on a plan to keep Rory out of the house while Mott went back inside and disposed of the Sea Bonnies. Mott had plenty of time to work on his plan because neither he nor Rory were particularly good at throwing or catching. A lot of time was spent running around their big backyard, chasing the ball.

Mott's house sat on a large lot, which backed up on a greenbelt. A thick forest of old oak and maple trees hugged the fence line, and gnarled branches reached into the yard to drop leaves. Uneven grass covered most of the yard. It used to be thick green grass, but when Mott's dad started taking longer flights, which kept him away longer, he stopped doing things like fertilizing and trimming. Moles started burrowing under the lawn, and the yard turned lumpy . . . sort of like Not Fritz.

Mott squinted up at the sun, which was starting to slide toward the horizon. He needed an excuse soon to keep Rory outside.

"Hey, Rory!" a child's voice called from the other side of the wooden fence at the north end of the yard.

"Hey, Danny!" Rory called back. He'd been running after the ball, but he abandoned that task and veered toward the wood slats that separated Rory's domain from Danny's.

"Wanna come play ball?" Rory shouted. He put his face up to one of the weathered fence boards and peered through a knothole.

"Nope!" Danny called. "Mom and I are taking Dapup for his first walk on a leash. Wanna come?"

"Yeah!" Rory shouted.

He turned to look at Mott. "Can we?" he yelled. He did a typical Rory spastic dance of excitement.

Mott grinned. This was perfect! He nodded. "You go ahead. I'll stay here and get started on my homework so I'll have more time to play with you later."

"Cool!" Rory shouted. He dropped his mitt and ran toward the gate.

"I'll keep an eye on them," Danny's mother called through the fence.

"Thanks, Mrs. Fairchild!"

Mott charged back into the house as soon as Rory slammed the gate shut and started shouting, "What's up, Dapup?"

Mott had a feeling a walk that included a puppy and two antsy boys wasn't going to be a long one. He needed to hurry.

He took the stairs two at a time and ran down the hall to Rory's room. Rory's door was open; it always was during the day. Inside the room, Mott went directly to Rory's desk, shoved aside a pile of books, and reached for the fish tank.

The sound of splashing water stopped him. He looked in the tank. Its lid was up, probably because Rory had forgotten to close it after he fed his little maniacal creatures. Mott could see both through the glass and from above the water that the Sea Bonnies were spun up, violently darting this way and that, creating swirls under the water and rough waves on the top. It was if they knew what he planned to do.

Yeah, well, so what? He wasn't going to have to be worried about what they knew and didn't know soon enough.

Mott strode to the desk, reached out, and slapped the fish tank lid closed. The water inside the tank churned more wildly. The lid vibrated, like it was going to pop open. Mott smacked his hand down on top of it, then used his other hand to put a book on the lid. He looked around and grabbed one of Rory's T-shirts off the floor. Covering the tank with the shirt—because he sure didn't want to look at the Sea Bonnies as he carried them to their deaths—he pulled the tank toward him and lifted it off the desk.

The sound of frothing water got louder. He ignored it.

The fish tank was a lot heavier than he expected it to be, but he was strong enough to carry it, barely. From this point, he had to go slowly.

He walked methodically and steadily toward the bathroom, and when he got there, he set the fish tank on the counter. He flipped on the light and closed the bathroom door. The toilet seat lid opened with a squeak.

Mott turned toward the fish tank. He had to take the T-shirt and the book off the tank now. He wished he had rubber gloves. He didn't want a single drop of the water in the fish tank to touch him.

Well, he'd just have to be careful.

Mott took off the fish tank's lid, inspected it for errant Sea Bonnies, found none, and set it aside. Then he ever so carefully began pouring the fish tank's water and the Sea Bonnies into the toilet bowl.

He half expected to hear whispering as he poured. Would the Sea Bonnies beg for their lives? Would they try to make him feel guilty or murderous?

He heard nothing. Maybe they were in shock. It was

a good thing they didn't try to make him feel bad because he felt no regret. What he felt was relief. Deep and profound relief.

He couldn't empty the entire fish tank into the toilet bowl at once, so he started by pouring as much of the water out as he could; while he poured, he flushed. Once he had most of the water gone, he was able to flush the bulk of the Sea Bonnies together. Then it took one last spill to dump the last of the Sea Bonnies and poor Not Fritz into the toilet.

He watched the remaining Sea Bonnies and Not Fritz whirl around the toilet bowl, and as soon as they disappeared and clear water refilled the bowl, he did a fist pump. "Yes!" he shouted.

He looked inside the fish tank to be sure all the Sea Bonnies were gone. They weren't.

One purplish creature was flopping around on the bottom of the tank. Mott quickly held the fish tank under the bathtub faucet. He let about an inch of water run into the tank, and he swished it around. Then he dumped this water, too. He flushed again. Checked the fish tank. No Sea Bonnies.

Moving fast again, Mott grabbed a roll of paper towels from under the sink. He also ran down to the kitchen to get his mom's big stockpot.

It had occurred to him while he was watching the Sea Bonnies head off to their sewer-y grave that he should have a plausible story for why he'd flushed his brother's "friends." He'd quickly come up with one. He was going to make it look like he'd been trying to clean the tank and, when he'd transferred them to the pot, they'd died . . . perhaps poisoned by the stainless steel? That should work. Rory wouldn't know any better. His mom probably wouldn't either. And she wouldn't care much. She had other things to think about. Even if Rory pitched a fit and went running to his mommy, his mom wouldn't suspect Mott of deliberately disposing of the Sea Bonnies. She'd just soothe Rory's hurt feelings, and that would be that.

Which was *almost* what happened. The only part of the scenario that didn't play out according to Mott's plan was Rory's reaction.

Rory didn't pitch a fit. He didn't throw a tantrum. He didn't go running to his mommy. Instead, he burst into tears, ran into his room, slammed the door, and locked it.

Okay, so maybe Mott felt a little bad. He loved his brother, and he didn't want to upset the little guy. Had there been some other way to handle the situation?

Mott stood outside his brother's door asking himself this question as he tried to get Rory to come downstairs for dinner. "I'm really sorry, buddy," he called through the closed door. "I was only trying to help."

This much was true. He'd been trying to help himself be free of the Sea Bonnies, for sure. But he also didn't like them being in the same room as his little brother. After all, the loathsome things did chow down on Fritz—they might be dangerous. What if they bit Rory and gave him an infection?

"Mom wants you to come down to dinner," Mott called through the closed door.

"Go away!" Rory yelled. "I'm not here."

"Um, okay," Mott said. "Then who's yelling at me?"

"Not me!" Rory shouted.

A chill skittered down Mott's spine. "Not me" was way too close to "Not Fritz." The image of a Sea Bonnie–infested Rory flashed through Mott's mind. He shuddered and stepped back from the door.

"Suit yourself," he called.

Mott fell into bed just before 10:00 p.m., exhausted. Not only had he slept very little the night before, he'd tapped out his energy with all the thinking he'd done during the day, the adrenaline rush of vanquishing his enemies, and the struggle to get Rory to open his bedroom door.

The latter part of Mott's tough day had stretched through the evening. Neither his nor his mom's powers of persuasion had been enough to get Rory to open his door. Eventually, it was Rory's need to pee that got his door open. When he finally came out and emptied his bladder, he made two announcements:

To his mom, he announced, "I'm hungry."

"I bet you are," she said. "That's what happens when you refuse to open your door." She pulled him close. "Why don't you come and climb in bed with me and you can explain to me why you did what you did and I can explain to you why you don't get to do it anymore?

If we're both satisfied at the end of the conversation, I'll fix you a snack. Deal?"

Rory wiped red eyes and nodded. He then turned to Mott and announced, "You're not my brother."

"Rory!" his mom admonished.

"It's okay, Mom," Mott said. "I get it." To Rory, he said, "I really am sorry."

That was only part of a lie. He wasn't sorry he'd flushed the Sea Bonnies, but he was sorry that Rory was upset.

Now Mott lay in the silent house and wondered if Rory had fallen asleep. Rory had still been crying when their mom put him to bed.

The house creaked, and outside an owl hooted. Mott turned on his side and looked at his curtain-covered window. His window looked out over the greenbelt behind the house, and it was right over the roof that covered the back deck. In the summer, he liked to climb out onto that roof and sit in the sun, watching the birds in the trees. It was so peaceful.

Mott closed his eyes. He realized he was relaxed for the first time since he'd seen the Sea Bonnies in Rory's tank. He exhaled and went to sleep. As soon as he did, he dropped into a dream.

Mott sat at the breakfast table, eating his cornflakes and reading the last of his English literature assignment. Shoveling in his food, keeping his eye on the pages of his book, he spooned up milk and flakes over and over. As he neared the bottom of the bowl, though, he shifted his gaze from the book to the cereal.

And that's when he saw them.

Instead of seeing flakes floating in his milk, Mott saw Sea Bonnies swimming in formation around his bowl. Their squidgy bluish bodies disgustingly pulsing through the milk, the Sea Bonnies flipped over and looked up at him with itty-bitty black beady eyes.

Mott yelled, gagged, and shoved the bowl away from him. "No!"

Mott's yell followed him out of his dream and into his waking state. He thrashed free of his covers and sat up. The hair on his arms was sticking out, and his heart was pounding hard and fast and loud in his chest. He felt a dry heave come up. He swallowed it down. He started to retch, and he sprang out of his bed and rushed to the bathroom.

Afraid his cry might have pulled his mom from a deep sleep, Mott didn't turn on the bathroom light. He didn't want her to worry. He groped in the dark for the glass he knew was next to the sink, ran tap water into the glass, and started chugging it down.

Halfway through the glass, the water going down Mott's throat suddenly felt clumpy, like it had thickened or it suddenly had something in it, like a glob of noodles in a bowl of chicken soup. Choking and sputtering, he dropped the glass as he reached for the light.

The light came on just as the glass landed in the sink and cracked. Mott quickly shut the bathroom door and scooped up the glass to examine it closely.

Holding the glass up to the light, he inspected the water droplets caught on the inside curve. Was anything swimming in the drops? He also studied the crack. Was anything caught in it?

He saw nothing but water.

Sitting on the closed toilet seat, he thought about what he'd felt in his throat. Had he really felt something, or had he just swallowed wrong? Maybe there had been some toothpaste in the glass? Or maybe his mind had conjured up the sensation because of his dream.

Given what he'd done that day, it was easy to assume he'd imagined feeling something slimy slip down his throat. As freaked out as he was by the Sea Bonnies, it was surprising he could even think about drinking water.

Mott picked up the cracked glass and looked at it again. Nope. Still nothing.

Mott blew out a sigh and headed back into his room.

When he opened his eyes the next morning, Mott's logic faced its first foe. His stomach was cramping so badly he could barely get out of bed and go to the bathroom to pee. And when he was done with that, it was all he could do to get back into the bed, curl onto his side, clutch his stomach, and moan.

That's where his mother found him when she came in to be sure he was up.

"Rise and shine!" she called out. "It's a—Mott?" She rushed to the side of the bed. "What's wrong?" She felt his forehead.

Mott hesitated. "I'm not sure. I have stomach cramps, like, big ones. I must have eaten something bad last night."

His mom frowned at him. "What did you eat that we didn't eat?"

That's the million-dollar question, isn't it? Mott thought.

"All I had yesterday was what you made me for lunch and what we had for dinner." As far as food went, that was the truth.

He wasn't about to tell her about thinking he'd swallowed a Sea Bonnie. That opened a can of worms—or Sea Bonnies—he didn't want to get into.

"I'll go get something for your stomach," his mom said. "And I'll check on Rory to be sure he's okay. Maybe he's sick, too, and that's why he was so upset about his Sea Bonnies last night."

Mott opened his mouth to respond, but another wave of cramping gripped his intestines. And right on the heels of that, the whispers returned.

Wuss, the little whispers flung at him. *Can't handle swallowing just one? What do you think a hundred would feel like? Two hundred? Two thousand?*

The whispers morphed into what sounded like hushed giggles, thousands of them.

Mott closed his eyes and pressed his lips together.

"I'll be right back," his mom said.

He heard his mom's footfalls tap across the floor. She was already dressed for work, wearing her high heels.

She must have an event today. And here he was making trouble for her.

Mott tried to concentrate on his breathing, but between the cramping and the whispers, he couldn't stay focused on it. He couldn't decide which was worse, the horrible cramping or the eerie and relentless whispers.

Serves you right, the whispers were saying now. *Every bad deed gets punished.*

Mott's mom reappeared with the chalky medicine she always gave him when his stomach was upset. "Rory's fine," she said, pouring Mott a dose.

He swallowed it dutifully.

"But he had a peanut butter sandwich yesterday," his mom said. "I gave you the rest of the lunch meat. It must have gone bad. I'm so, so sorry, honey!"

"It's not your fault, Mom," he said, absolutely meaning it.

He had no doubt whatsoever that the way he felt had nothing to do with bad lunch meat. It had to do with what had gone down his throat last night. He was sure of it. Convincing himself he'd swallowed Rory's toothpaste had been wishful thinking.

You're not as stupid as you look, the whispering voices said.

Mott looked up at his mom. "I think I just need to go back to sleep. Maybe when I wake up, I'll feel better."

He was lying now, to both himself and his mom.

"Are you sure? I could"—she chewed on her lower lip—"have someone else run the event—"

"No, Mom, you don't need to do that. I'll be fine."

She felt his forehead again. "You're not hot. In fact, you're kind of on the cool side."

"Chocolate milk!" Rory shouted from the hallway. "I want chocolate milk for breakfast!"

Mott cringed at the volume. His mom gave him a half smile. "Well, apparently he's gotten over his upset."

"Good," Mott said.

"Mom!" Rory yelled.

"I'm coming," she called.

She looked at Mott one more time. "You're sure you—?"

"I'll be fine," he lied again. He wasn't at all sure he was going to be fine.

The cramps were starting to feel more intense, and the voices were getting more insistent. The whispering wasn't a unison murmur anymore. It was more like the garbled hissing of hundreds of voices all muttering at once. He could no longer make out whole phrases, but he caught a word here and there. *Stupid* was used frequently. He also heard *guilty* and *murderer* a few times. Once, he was sure he heard *milksop*.

"Did you hear me?" his mom asked.

"What?" Mott curled up tighter as a new spasm clutched at his belly.

"I said that if you don't feel better when you wake

up, be sure to call Ron. I'm going to get on the phone with him before I leave and tell him you might be needing him."

Ron was Dr. T. That was actually a good idea. Mott said so, and then he closed his mouth on the groan that wanted to erupt into the room.

In the hallway, Rory shouted, "I'm starving!"

His mom leaned over and kissed Mott on the forehead. "Sleep, honey. You'll feel better soon."

She crossed to the door, gave him one last look, and left the room. He heard her talking softly to Rory in the hallway. Then he heard Rory's footsteps pounding down the stairs and his mom's tapping heels after that.

Mott closed his eyes and tried to sleep.

Tried being the operative word.

When Mott looked at his bedside digital clock for the 761st time—okay, maybe he hadn't looked quite that many times, but close—at 1:37 in the afternoon, precisely, he gave up trying to convince himself he was going to feel better soon. It just wasn't going to happen.

At 1:38, he got up and went into the bathroom. He thought maybe if he could use the toilet, he'd feel better.

Five minutes later, he was back in his bedroom. And he wasn't feeling better. Moaning, he changed into sweats, a T-shirt, and some athletic shoes. He called Dr. T's clinic.

Claudia, Dr. T's receptionist, answered. Mott could

picture her holding the phone as they spoke. Large and cushy with wildly curly hair and kind hazel eyes, Claudia was a caring woman Mott had known as long as he'd known Dr. T. She immediately put Dr. T on the phone.

"Can you get over here on your own?" Dr. T asked.

"I think . . . I can bike . . . over," Mott struggled to get out.

His hesitations weren't entirely caused by stomach cramps. The whispers were getting louder, and they were as distracting as all get-out. What he was hearing sounded kind of like someone quickly scanning through radio stations; however, he was hearing snatches of words and phrases instead of snatches of songs. None of them were anything he wanted to listen to.

". . . in about fifteen minutes," Dr. T said.

"I'm sorry. What?"

"I said your voice and your hesitations aren't giving me a lot of confidence in your biking abilities. Claudia's going on her lunch break, and she said she'll swing over to get you. She'll be there in about fifteen minutes."

"Oh, I don't want to—"

"Don't argue with your doctor," Dr. T said. He chuckled.

Mott sighed. "Thank you."

One of the voices whispered, *Sucker.*

Dr. T had exam rooms designed to please the various age groups he focused on. He had some for the little kids, the grade-school kids, and the teens. Unfortunately, because Dr. T was squeezing in Mott between other patients, Mott landed in a little-kid room. So, when he lay on his back, he was staring up at a ceiling painted with sparkly rainbows, flying purple pigs, and a blue-tinged Pegasus that at the moment resembled a Sea Bonnie far more than it should have. It must have been the wings, which looked vaguely like bunny ears. And that purplish-blue color. He never really wanted to see that color again.

Mott quickly looked away from the ceiling, turning his head to gaze at the room's walls. They were painted yellow and covered with animal stencils. Pretty much every imaginable animal had a spot in the room, including a rabbit, which Mott could have sworn was staring at him with animosity.

Mott closed his eyes. The paper beneath him crinkled as he shifted to find a semi-comfortable position while Dr. T prodded his belly. Every time Dr. T asked, "Does this hurt?" Mott gasped, "Yes."

Dr. T stepped back and sat on his rolling stool. Mott heard the vinyl squeak, and the rollers rattle as Dr. T scooted over to the laptop he'd set up at a small counter next to the exam table.

Dr. T was kind of a funny-looking guy; this was mostly caused by his big ears and his equally large nose, but a goatee that came to a point under his chin contributed, too. On top of these eye-catching features, he was short and totally bald; when Mott and Nate were ten, Dr. T had shaved what little remained of his light brown hair. He looked a bit like one of the seven dwarfs or maybe a gnome.

He might have been one of the nicest people Mott had ever met, though, even nicer than Mott's mom. His mom occasionally lost her temper. Dr. T never did.

Mott tried to concentrate on how nice Dr. T was, but the whispered voices got louder. He was now hearing more full sentences.

You don't know what you're dealing with, for example, came through clearly.

Mott tried to keep his breathing steady while he watched Dr. T type. He felt sweat trickle down between his shoulder blades, and he squirmed.

He was attempting to stay calm, but these cramps and the relentless whispers were terrifying. What was happening inside his body?

Mott abruptly rose up on an elbow. He glanced at his belly, and he frowned. Did his belly look lumpy? He thought it did.

"Okay," Dr. T said. "Here's what we're going to do. I'm going to get Louise in here to draw some blood. The blood tests will tell me if you have an infection. When she's done with that, Louise will also do an ultrasound. That will tell me if we're looking at a gall-bladder issue, which is a possibility."

Mott nodded. He didn't bother to ask questions about his gallbladder. He pointed at his belly. "Do you think my stomach looks lumpy? I think it looks lumpy."

Dr. T stood and looked down at Mott's stomach. "It looks normal to me, and I didn't feel any masses."

Mott frowned. "Okay."

Dr. T patted Mott's thigh. "When you feel like crap, it's easy for the mind to start imagining all kinds of worst-case scenarios. So, let's start your treatment right away, even while we get the tests set up."

"What treatment?"

Dr. T flipped his computer screen, turning it into a tablet. He tapped the screen and handed it to Mott. "Watch this. Louise will be here in a few minutes to draw blood and do the ultrasound." Dr. T pressed a button, and the upper part of the table Mott lay on raised a little. "That work?"

Mott nodded. He took the tablet.

Dr. T patted his leg again. "I'll be back after I look at your tests. In the meantime"—he pointed at the tablet screen Mott held—"watch that."

Dr. T strode from the room, closing the door behind him. Mott, cringing at another round of cramping, looked at the screen. It was frozen on a video of a stand-up comic routine.

He managed a half smile and shook his head. Leave it to Dr. T to "prescribe" laughter.

Maybe the laughter helped.

Mott had been tempted to set aside Dr. T's tablet and just be miserable while he waited for Louise, but two more intense cramps and a whispered *Your time is coming*, got him to hit "Play" on the screen.

He hadn't heard of the comedian in the video, but he was really funny. Mott managed to chuckle at first, and then he was actually laughing so hard that Louise, a small dark-haired woman in a ponytail, had to pause the video while she took blood. She let him watch again while she did the ultrasound, which she did silently.

After a few minutes of feeling her pressing her "magic wand," as she called it, all over his stomach, Mott asked, "Do you see anything?"

"I don't, kiddo," she said. "But we'll have Dr. T come in and give a look-see to be sure."

The look-see came quickly. Dr. T studied the scan and grinned at Mott. "Everything looks normal."

"Really?" Mott frowned. "Then why do I feel so bad?"

"Honestly, I'm not one hundred percent sure, but my guess is you have food poisoning. I'll know more when I get your bloodwork. But nothing horrible is going on."

Mott nodded. "Okay."

Dr. T squeezed his shoulder. "Your enthusiasm is overwhelming." He chuckled. "How about this? Why don't you get dressed and go hang out on the sofa in my office? I have a couple more patients to see. Then I'm heading home. I'll give you a ride."

Mott nodded again.

When Dr. T and Louise left the room, Mott sat up on the edge of the exam table and took in what Dr. T had said. He tried believing it.

"You're fine," he told himself out loud.

Liar, liar, pants on fire, the whispers countered.

Mott shook his head and stood up to get dressed. "You're not real," he said to the whispers. "I'm fine."

Although he could have sworn that he heard sibilant laughter in his head, Mott ignored it and got dressed. Strangely, the cramping had abated a little. Maybe it was the laughter, but it was more likely the power of suggestion. He was comforted by the results of the ultrasound. If something foreign had been in his belly, the scan would have found it, right?

Right.

Mott was able to walk semi-normally down the clinic's hallway. Behind the purple-and-white-striped door of exam room 2, near Dr. T's office, a little girl giggled. Mott smiled. It was a nice sound, much nicer than the poisonous murmurs in his head. He pushed open the door of Dr. T's office and dropped onto Dr. T's overstuffed blue-and-yellow polka-dot couch. Listening to the continued giggling, he fell asleep.

He woke only long enough for Dr. T to walk him out to Dr. T's new SUV and get him home. Then he went up to his bed, and he fell back asleep.

When Mott woke up, it was dark, but the dark wasn't nighttime dark—it was predawn dark. He sat up. He'd slept for over twelve hours!

Taking stock, he realized he felt . . . okay. His stomach was sore, but he wasn't cramping like before.

The whispers were still in his head, but they seemed muted. ·

Fumbling for his small bedside lamp, Mott switched it on. As soon as the light poured onto his nightstand, he saw a bottle of water, several crackers in a plastic bag, and a note. He picked up the note.

Mott, you were sleeping soundly, and Ron said that was the best thing for you, so I didn't wake you. I've left you some crackers in case you wake up hungry. If you need me, come and get me! I love you. Mom

Mott smiled and reached for the bottled water. He was really thirsty, so he quickly unscrewed the lid. He started to bring the bottle to his lips, but then he stopped. He held the bottle under the glow of his lamp, and he studied it.

He rolled his eyes. It was just water. Bottled water in a sealed container. It was fine.

He drank some water, and he reached for the crackers. Leaning back on his pillows, he opened the plastic bag and plucked out a whole wheat cracker. Munching on it, he looked around his semi-dark room—at the nature posters and photos of his favorite baseball stadiums, at the shelves full of video games and math puzzle books, at the closet he knew was stuffed with his clothes and hiking and fishing gear. He took comfort in being reminded of who he was.

He wasn't Mott, a boy infested by Sea Bonnies. He was Mott, lover of baseball and video games and math and camping out, best friend to Nate and Lyle, a good brother to Rory . . . and maybe soon-to-be boyfriend to Theresa. He was a normal teen.

You're a freak, the whispers countered.

"Yeah, and you're not real," he told them. In the light of this new day it felt even more true. He shook his head—Sea Bonnies couldn't even hatch without purified water above seventy-five degrees—how were they going to survive his stomach acid? He chuckled as he kept munching on crackers and looking around his room.

Over Mott's desk, opposite his bed, he had a dark green bulletin board covered in photos. The photos represented his favorite things and best memories. The one in the middle was a picture of him and his dad sitting in a rowboat in the middle of the lake where his family had a summer cabin. His dad always got a couple weeks off in July, and they went to the cabin to swim and hike and fish. Mott usually felt disconnected from his dad, but when they fished, he felt close to—

Fish.

Mott dropped his half-eaten cracker and sat up.

His reminiscing had reminded him of Fritz, the fish that was no longer a fish when Mott flushed it down the toilet with the Sea Bonnies. He hadn't imagined the way Not Fritz had looked when Mott had last seen him.

He might have been imagining the whispers, but he'd seen what he'd seen. Fritz had been eaten from the inside out and replaced by Sea Bonnies. He was pretty sure fish had stomach acid, too, and yet the Sea Bonnies had still managed to get him.

Mott looked down at his belly. Setting aside the plate, he raised his shirt with a trembling hand. He put his palm against his skin.

It was normal. Wasn't it?

Mott thought about how horrible he'd felt the day before and how he felt now. He'd assumed the end of his cramps was a good thing. But what if all that meant was that the Sea Bonnies had finished their work on his stomach?

Maybe he felt better because his belly was no longer being consumed. It was now something else—his not belly.

Mott gingerly felt all over his stomach. Did it feel different than it used to? More gelatinous?

Mott groaned and swiped the bag of crackers off his lap. They hit the floor with a muffled crunch, and Mott slid all the way under his covers, pulling them up over his head.

He wanted to escape, to hide from the world. No, what he wanted was to hide from the Sea Bonnies . . . and from himself.

You can't hide, the whispers told him.

"Yeah?" Mott said. "Watch me."

Mott covered his ears and started humming.

That's where his mom found him—under his covers, humming like a little kid—when she came into his room, still in her robe, to check on him.

"Mott?"

He threw back the covers and looked at her.

Apparently, he looked worse than he felt. As soon as her gaze landed on his face, she frowned and said, "You're staying home again today."

He didn't argue with her.

After his mom and Rory left the house, Mott dropped back into sleep, but he didn't stay asleep for long. This was unfortunate . . . because as soon as he was awake, his mind was inundated by the whispers again.

The whispers in Mott's head, however, were no longer whispers. They were full-on shouts.

If he didn't drown them out, he was going to lose his mind.

Mott threw back his covers and dashed to his desk to get his earbuds. Putting them in, he started filling his ears with driving rock music.

He could still hear the shouts. What could he do? He looked around. His gaze landing on his shelves, he reached out and picked up one of his handheld video games. He got back under the covers, and he turned on the game. Mott spent the better part of the day trying to drown out the shouts, but not even deafening rock music and fast-moving video games could beat them down.

Then, sometime during the afternoon, maybe a little after 2:00 p.m., Mott started feeling odd. When he stopped his game to figure out why he felt that way, he realized he had a strange vibration in his chest and belly. It was like the very faintest suggestion of movement, as if something was shaking his organs from the inside. He felt like his heart was . . . quivering. And his lungs felt curiously unstable every time he took a breath, like instead of expanding and contracting they kind of . . . wiggled, struggling not to collapse.

He couldn't stand this anymore. He had to get another scan.

Mott picked up the phone and called Dr. T's cell phone. He didn't want to go through Claudia.

"Hello? This is Dr. Tabor."

Mott gripped the phone. "Dr. T? This is Mott."

"Hey, Mott. How are you feeling this morning?"

"Um, that's the thing. I still feel weird."

"Still cramping?"

"Not so much cramping as, um, like shaking on the inside, like my organs are, um, trembling."

For four seconds—Mott counted—the only thing he heard through the phone was the faintest of hisses in the line. Then Dr. T said, "Let's do this. I'm on my way over to the hospital to visit a couple patients before I head home for a while. I need to go back in late tonight to work on inventory with Claudia, so I'm leaving the clinic early. Why don't I stop by and get you? We'll see if we can squeeze you in for a CAT scan. Shouldn't be a problem. Given what you're telling me, I can get insurance approval for it. Do you want me to talk to your mom before I come over?"

"I'll do it," Mott said quickly. He didn't want to worry his mother.

Dr. T was quiet for another few seconds. "Okay. I'll talk to her later. After the scan."

"That would be good."

As soon as he hung up the phone, Mott scribbled a note for his mom on the back of the note she'd left for him, just in case she got home before he did. The note was filled with lies, but the truth was out of the question. What was he supposed to write? *Mom, I've gone to get a scan to see if Sea Bonnies are eating me from the inside out.* No, that wouldn't be a good idea.

He settled with an evasive lie:

Mom, I'm feeling better. Gone out to get some fresh air. Will call later. Love you. Mott

Mott sat in front of Dr. T's small oak desk in his clinic's office. Dr. T was on the phone talking to another doctor, one who had analyzed the CAT scan.

Mott wasn't listening to what Dr. T was saying. He didn't really care at this point. He'd already heard enough from Dr. T himself.

Now he was just trying to stay calm. So, he was leaning forward, his elbows on his knees, and he was staring at his shoes. There was a brown speck on one of his white athletic shoes. He was using it as a focal point, concentrating on it the way a seasoned meditator might stare at a candle. He wondered if he should try a mantra or maybe an om. He needed something to tether him to sanity because the facts were dragging him quickly toward madness.

Apparently, the scan had revealed "abnormalities" in Mott's stomach, intestines, lungs, and heart. They looked "variegated" in a way that was "inconsistent with normal tissue."

Dr. T and the other doctor were now discussing potential causes of the abnormalities. Were they tumors? Were they evidence of some sort of systemic infection? No and no. The doctors knew of no biological cause that could be responsible for the scan's results.

Mott didn't care about the discussion because he already knew what had caused the "variegated" appearance of his organs. He'd seen it as soon as Dr. T had shown Mott his scan.

"Here's what the CAT scan revealed," Dr. T had said, tapping a few keys on his laptop to bring up the images of Mott's scan.

Dr. T had pointed to light-colored clumps clustered together all through Mott's intestines, his stomach, his lungs, and his heart. The clumps were grayish-white, and they had small dark specks sprinkled throughout. At first glance, the specks appeared to be random, but when Mott had leaned closer to Dr. T's computer screen, it was obvious the specks weren't haphazard. No. The specks came in pairs. And they weren't specks. They were eyes. If you really studied the clumps, you could see they were made up of elongated forms, each vaguely rabbit-shaped, each with two dark dots.

Mott had almost thrown up when he'd seen the truth of what was going on inside him. But for some reason, he hadn't been able to. He'd gagged, but nothing had come up.

Dr. T hung up the phone, steepled his fingers, and looked at Mott across his desk. "Dr. Jenkins and I agree that the scan's anomalies don't fit anything seen before. That's a good thing. It means that the scan's results are likely caused by an issue with the scan itself, interference with the machine. He suggested we repeat the scan tomorrow morning, and I think that's a good idea."

Mott tore his gaze away from the brown spot on his shoe. He looked at Dr. T.

Ignoring the rippling sensation that he felt in his chest, he said, "We don't need to repeat the scan. I know what it is."

He was shocked by how calm he sounded. His words were totally flat, too flat, actually. He sounded a little like a robot, but that was just because he was too stunned to bother with putting inflection in his words.

Dr. T frowned at Mott. "What do you think it is, Mott? Is there something you haven't told me?"

Mott figured Dr. T thought Mott had taken something he shouldn't have taken. In a way, he had . . . but not on purpose.

Mott shook his head. "No. I mean *yes*. But it's not what you think."

Dr. T raised his eyebrows and waited.

"The thing is," Mott said, scooting forward in his seat, "a few days ago, Rory got some Sea Bonnies from Freddy Fazbear's Pizzeria."

Dr. T frowned a question.

"They're kind of like sea monkeys," Mott said. "You know? Those brine shrimp things?"

Dr. T nodded.

"A couple of days after they hatched," Mott continued, "I noticed that Fritz, Rory's goldfish, which shared the tank with the Sea Bonnies, didn't look right. When I really looked at him closely, I saw that he was no longer a goldfish; it was like the Sea Bonnies had eaten him from the inside out—infested him."

Mott could tell from Dr. T's blank expression that Mott was losing him. When Dr. T opened his mouth to speak, Mott started talking faster, almost running his words together the same way Rory did when he got excited. "That's what made me realize I had to get rid of the things, which I did. I flushed them. And Rory was all upset. But later that night, I got a drink of water, and I felt something go down my throat, and I tried to convince myself it wasn't a Sea Bonnie, but now I think it was. And I think it started eating my tissue, and it multiplied and now my insides are turning into Sea Bonnies, the same way Fritz turned into Sea Bonnies. They're eating me from the inside, and they're coming together to replace my organs. I think that's why I feel so weird on the inside, like I'm jiggling from within, like gelatin sort of, but not exactly."

Mott stopped talking. He concentrated on breathing in and out, which for obvious reasons, was becoming harder than usual. He tried not to think about masses of Sea Bonnies roiling around together to form the walls of his lungs.

Dr. T took a deep breath. "It's time to call your mom."

Mott slumped in his chair.

Several hours later, near midnight, Mott sat on the edge of his bed. Once again, he was staring at the brown spot on his shoe.

He'd been staring at his shoe for a long time, an abnormally long time. He was staring at it mostly because he didn't know what else to do.

He stared at it through the better part of the evening, listening to Rory chatter at his mom, listening to his mom trying to get Rory to calm down and go to bed, listening to Rory finally settle into his room, listening to his mom's footsteps pause outside Mott's door and then continue on to her room. Obviously, she'd decided to deal with him in the morning.

Outside, thunder rumbled. Finally, the weather suited the situation.

When they'd left the clinic earlier in the evening, Mott had noticed the ozone smell in the air, and he'd turned his face up to the soft rain starting to fall. For an instant, it had soothed him. But just for an instant. A streak of jagged lightning on the horizon had brought him back to his intolerable reality. Nothing he was facing could be eased by a little bit of rain.

Now the rain matched how Mott felt. It wasn't soft or soothing. It was angry and insistent. He could hear it thrumming on the roof, assaulting the house like thousands of jackhammers trying to drill through the shingles.

When Mott's mom had brought him home and asked him to go up to his room, she'd followed him as far as his doorway. Then she'd said, in the strained voice she used when she was trying to remain calm but wanted to scream hysterically, "Please stay in here. We'll talk . . . later."

For hours, Mott had been thinking about what that talk would be like. How would he convince her he wasn't crazy? Did he even want to try?

Wouldn't it be better if he *was* crazy? When you weighed the pros and cons, crazy was definitely the preferred scenario. If he was crazy, the worst that could happen was that he might get put in a mental hospital for a while. Maybe he'd have to do group therapy, talk about his feelings, and eat yucky tapioca pudding. But he'd be Mott. He'd be Mott, made up of his own parts, a human. Normal.

The alternative to crazy was being Not Mott. Absolutely unable to forget what Not Fritz had looked like, Mott knew that when the Sea Bonnies were done with him, if they were consuming him from the inside, Mott wouldn't be anything remotely resembling a human. And that meant Mott's life would be over.

He wanted to convince himself he was going crazy. He really did. But the problem with that was the CAT scan. He wasn't the only person who'd seen something weird on the scan. Dr. T had seen it, and so had the other doctor. They hadn't seen Sea Bonnies, of course, because their minds didn't let them entertain something so absurd, something so outside the bounds of what science understood to be possible. But they had seen something. Mott wasn't imagining the physical changes in his body.

This was a very worrying fact.

Mott felt an itch on his forearm, and he idly scratched it. It still itched. He scratched harder.

When the spot kept itching, he looked down at his arm. And there, where it itched, something moved just under his skin.

Mott stood up so fast he got dizzy and immediately collapsed back onto the bed. He swallowed hard and stared at his arm. Yes, there—the faintest of elongated lumps were slithering under the surface of his skin.

Mott groaned. His whole forearm started to itch, and he scratched at it so hard that he broke the skin. In horror, he stared at the blood welling up. Flicking up through that blood, the tail of a Sea Bonnie squirmed in the thick redness. His eyes nearly bugging out of his head, Mott watched the Sea Bonnie tail disappear as the Sea Bonnie dove back down under his skin.

If he could have sawed his arm off and thrown it away, he would have.

His whole arm itched now, and he could see that the movement was all up and down his arm. Not only that, his skin was changing color. Right in front of his eyes, his skin was losing its normal pigment.

It was becoming translucent. And it was turning a pale shade of purple blue.

Mott looked at his other arm. The same thing was happening to it.

For several seconds, Mott didn't move. Not at all. He wasn't even sure he was breathing. He became a statue—a frozen collection of mutating cells overseen by a brain incapable of accepting the impossible transformation. Because this had to be impossible. He could not be sitting here watching Sea Bonnies eat his skin from underneath.

He was not seeing them take bite after bite of his cells, ingesting and integrating what used to be part of him and turning it into more of them. He was not being devoured and replaced by Sea Bonnies.

This. Was. Not. Real.

Maybe there was something wrong with his eyes. Maybe he was hallucinating.

Suddenly able to move, as if released from some paralytic drug or an evil magic spell, Mott jumped to his feet and ran to his dresser. Leaning over the top of it, pushing aside his deodorant and his hairbrush, he peered into his own eyes in the mirror.

And he saw a Sea Bonnie swim through the white surrounding his left iris. Then he saw two wind around the darker flecks of the brown in his right iris.

Mott lost what was left of his grip on reality. He ran

for his door, intending to flee the house. But he stopped when he heard his mother's voice in the hallway. He couldn't face her like this.

What if he infected her?

He needed to get back to Dr. T. Now that it was obvious what was happening to Mott, maybe Dr. T could help him. Dr. T had said he was going back to his clinic to work that night. Mott had to get to the clinic.

Mott whirled and raced to his window. Throwing it open, he popped the screen and climbed out into the night, onto the roof of the deck. Immediately, the rain stung his skin and his eyes. He didn't care.

He crawled quickly to the edge of the porch roof, and he bent over to grab the top of a downspout. Not concerned about cutting his hands, Mott wrapped them around the metal and swung his legs over the edge of the roof. Grasping the gutter spout with his arms and legs, he slid down it like a fireman's pole, and he hit the ground hard.

His ankle turned, and pain shot up his leg. But he ignored it. He also ignored the pain throbbing in his hands.

Mott looked out into the darkness extending behind his house. Why hadn't he brought a flashlight?

Well, maybe because he was a little distracted by being eaten by Sea Bonnies? That was a reasonable excuse.

Between the night and the rain coming down in almost solid walls of water, it was nearly impossible to see.

That was okay. He knew his yard, and he knew the forest behind it. He'd find his way.

He could have gone out to the sidewalk, where streetlights could show him the way, but he didn't want to be by the street. There were too many cars with bright headlight beams he didn't want to be caught in.

So Mott sloshed through the grass in his yard, and he scaled the fence at the back. He figured he could follow the greenbelt through his neighborhood. He knew if he stuck to the relatively narrow band of trees, they'd eventually lead him back to Dr. T's clinic. It was just a mile or so away. He could walk it.

Mott was so drenched by the time he reached the trees that his clothes clung to him like they were part of him. Or maybe they were part of the Sea Bonnies now.

Light from the houses along the greenbelt reached into the forest, enough so Mott could see that the ground was covered with standing water. Huge puddles had formed in the spongy loam under the old trees. The water was getting caught up in the depressions between vast root systems stretching through the underbrush.

Mott ran through the puddles and stumbled over knobby roots, occasionally falling against a rough tree trunk. As he ran, he scratched at his arms, which still itched incessantly, intensely. He couldn't stop digging at himself.

Not long after Mott left his house—he didn't know

how long because time was becoming something that made no sense to him—Mott scratched hard at his bicep, and when he pulled his hand away, he saw, in the yellow glow from someone's porch light, that he'd torn out a huge chunk of his own flesh.

No, not his own flesh.

When Mott looked at what he held in his hand, he recoiled, staggering back into the branches of an old oak tree. Instead of embracing him, the twigs prodded and speared him, but that didn't matter.

Nothing mattered but the fact that Mott was holding a handful of madly swimming Sea Bonnies instead of the flesh he thought he'd pulled away from his arm. Sickened, Mott flung the swimming creatures to the ground. He started to hurry on, but he noticed the Sea Bonnies were swimming energetically, coming together in an organized school to follow the rivulets from one puddle to the next. He stopped and stared, then realized they were swimming after him.

They were *pursuing* him.

Mott took off. He started reeling through the trees, zigging this way and that—not just to avoid the trees but to evade the Sea Bonnies coming after him.

He wished he could hear them advancing so he knew where they were. He knew better than to stop and turn to see them. They'd catch up if he did.

But he couldn't hear them. Mott could hear nothing but the staccato rhythm of the rain and his own rapid breathing.

He managed about ten ungainly strides over the uneven ground before he tripped and went down onto one knee. As soon as he did, the Sea Bonnies were there. He couldn't see them, but he could *feel* them. They immediately swam up his jeans and found their way to his arms, where they reattached themselves. Mott could feel his body reabsorbing the wriggling creatures.

He also realized he could feel the Sea Bonnies all through his body now. They were in every vein, every artery, every organ, every nerve . . . every system in his entire body. They were everywhere.

Mott turned his face to the sky, and he screamed. He screamed out his fear, his disbelief, and his rage. He screamed at the insanity of it all. He screamed because what else could he do but scream? He didn't know how to fight this battle. He didn't understand it. He couldn't even believe it. He was also pretty sure he'd already lost it.

But then again, maybe it wasn't too late. Maybe Dr. T could help him. Mott had to get to the clinic.

Mott started running again, squinting to see through the rain and the trees. He wiped his eyes, but instead of clearing his vision, this just swiped away another glop of Sea Bonnies. He flicked it off his fingers, and in the glow from someone's pool lights, he could see it hit a tree branch. Immediately, the Sea Bonnies slithered down the trunk, found a narrow channel of water between two roots, and followed it back to Mott. He felt the Sea Bonnies slip up his shin as he kept running.

Finally, Mott reached the end of the greenbelt. He careened off one last tree, and he stepped out onto the rain-pounded sidewalk that led to the back door of the clinic.

No, that wasn't right. He didn't actually *step* out. He flopped out. He couldn't step anymore because he was constantly coming apart. With every motion he made, pieces of his flesh fell away and turned into a heaving swell of Sea Bonnies, which swam chaotically and then coalesced into a formation that once again sought their fellows . . . and they, of course, were in Mott.

Not Mott.

Mott wasn't Mott anymore, and he knew it. He tried to dismantle himself. He pulled at his cheeks, at his ears, at his arms, at his chest, at his hips. He tore off handfuls of his flesh and tissue, throwing them aside. He realized some remote part of his brain—maybe a part not yet infested by Sea Bonnies—thought that if he could tear enough of himself away, he might unearth the few cells of Mott that were still Mott.

But each time Mott discarded parts of himself, the parts became determined masses of Sea Bonnies that doggedly found a way back to him, reattaching and reassimilating faster each time he tried to toss them. They were now doing that so powerfully that Mott even heard a sound when they came rushing back to him. It was a *slurp*, kind of like sucking the last bit of milkshake up through a straw. But that description was too benign. The Sea Bonnies weren't benign. They were malevolent through and through. All the Sea Bonnies wanted to do was vanquish every aspect of Mott. They wanted to vanquish him and conquer him. They wanted to be more than a colony; they wanted to be an empire—an empire formerly known as Mott.

No matter what Mott did to resist them, the Sea Bonnies retaliated and resurged. They filled back in every hole created by his self-demolition efforts. When the chunks of flesh Mott lobbed away hit the ground, they immediately separated into swimming Sea Bonnies, which began returning to Mott. To get to him, they followed the standing water on the ground. They used the puddles. They even took advantage of falling raindrops. Any and all water became a conduit leading the Sea Bonnies back to Mott.

Once they reached him, the Sea Bonnies sought any ingress they could find. They swam up his pant legs. They slithered around his shirt. They wriggled over his shoes. They returned to themselves, and their version of Mott, every single time.

As Mott fought this battle, he'd managed to get around the outside of the clinic. He was now close to the front door. Collapsing every few seconds as he attempted to extract parts of himself only to have them re-form immediately afterward, Mott realized he had very little time left.

He realized his thoughts were not really thoughts anymore. They were fragments. He was having trouble thinking of the people he cared about—his mom,

Rory, his friends, and . . . Theresa. He tried to conjure images of them in his head, but he could only see pieces of them. Soon, he'd no longer be anything like what he used to be. How much time did he have? Maybe minutes. Maybe seconds. Of the trillions of cells that had originally made up Mott, he figured only a few thousand were still as they'd been before the Sea Bonnie invasion.

Mott managed the last few feet to the clinic door. He reached for it . . . only to have his hand disintegrate in front of him and drop to the wet concrete.

Claudia looked up from her computer screen, out through the darkened waiting room to the blackness beyond the clinic's windows. The clinic was hushed and still, and perhaps because it was so quiet, in spite of the storm, she could hear something odd outside. It was kind of like a splashing sound, but not a normal rain spattering the ground sound. It was a bigger sound than that. It sounded like something large and squishy was falling into a body of water now and then.

What Claudia heard between the splashes was odd, too. She heard a sort of suctioning sound, almost a whistling. This was similar to the weird noise her vacuum made whenever she accidently sucked up something wet.

After the third time she heard that sound, Claudia decided to look outside the clinic to see what might be causing the peculiar noises. Making sure her computer was secure, Claudia stood and walked through the hushed waiting room.

Hesitating for a couple seconds by the door—and not sure why—Claudia eventually pushed the heavy glass door open. She peered out into the deluge and saw . . . Mott.

Mott stood there as if standing in heavy rain was a perfectly normal thing to do. The rain sluiced over his brown hair, which was matted to his head. It ran down his face, and it pattered against his clothing.

Claudia wasn't sure what to make of this. She decided to act the same way Mott was acting . . . as if everything was normal.

"Well, hello, Mott," Claudia said. She kept her expression neutral.

Claudia had known Mott since he was a baby. He was a nice boy, never a problem at the clinic. He'd been in yesterday and this morning, she knew. She didn't know why. Dr. T didn't discuss his patients with Claudia, even when the patient was almost part of the family.

Mott didn't look particularly healthy, though. He had an unnatural bluish tint, and he was so pale he was almost see-through.

When Mott didn't respond to her, Claudia asked, "Are you okay?"

Suddenly, Mott smiled. "Yes. It's a nice day. Everyone should be outside."

Again, Claudia was a little nonplussed. She leaned

forward to look in Mott's eyes. She was checking to see if his pupils looked okay. They did. She smiled at him.

He smiled back. Then he turned and walked away into the rain.

Claudia tried to see where he was going. She thought maybe she should call him back. But it was too late. The rain was coming down so relentlessly that once Mott was a few feet away, he seemed to disappear.

"I think a queen should have servants," Jessica said as she glided to her locker and struck a pose. She examined her bright-red nails. "I shouldn't be expected to do things like open lockers, especially when these old locks get stuck all the time. Remember last week? When I chipped a nail, right after I had that zebra polish put on? Remember, Brittany?"

"How could I not? It was tragic!" Brittany stared at her own nails, painted purple with gold swirls. She glowered at the combination lock on Jessica's locker. "I really think the principal should do something about getting, like, maintenance to replace your lock, especially now that you've been named homecoming queen."

"I know, right? Royalty should come with privileges."

"For sure," Brittany agreed as she opened her own locker next to Jessica's.

Jessica scanned the long gray-linoleum-floored

hallway to see who was looking at her and her best friend. Kids getting ready to go to class packed in tight around the scarred maroon lockers, chattering and shouting. Lockers slammed. Athletic shoes squeaked on the floor. The air was filled with energy and familiar smells: the pine-scented cleaners the janitorial staff had used at night, the cooking aromas drifting down the hall from the cafeteria staff's early preparations, and the occasional rank fart that some crude boy (it *had* to be a boy) let loose. Everyone was busy, but that didn't mean they were oblivious. They still noticed Jessica and Brittany.

Jessica knew that she and Brittany were the prettiest girls in their class, arguably in the entire school—which was why they were voted homecoming queen and homecoming princess even though they were just sophomores.

It had been a delicious controversy when the votes came in. The two seniors claimed the vote was rigged since there was no way they hadn't been the ones chosen. They demanded a recount, which came out in Jessica's and Brittany's favor. They were the royalty. There was no arguing about it.

Since then, Jessica and Brittany had been getting even more attention than was usual for them. Take this morning, for instance. Right now, several freshman girls stared at them from across the hall. Two nerdy guys practically drooled over them as they loped by.

Jessica never tired of watching her classmates ogle her and Brittany. They all did, boys and girls. Even the teachers stared.

Who wouldn't stare? Jessica and Brittany had it all—the shiny blonde hair, the big blue eyes, the high cheekbones, the pert noses, the full lips, the perfect petite figures, and the most up-to-date fashions and makeup to complement all their natural superiority. They were peacocks in a sea of pigeons. Everyone loved to admire their awesome feathers.

And they were looking particularly dope today. Over the weekend, they'd hit the sales at the mall and had gotten an amazing deal on the faux suede miniskirts they wore. The skirts weren't identical, of course—that would be the peak of lame. Jessica's tawny skirt buttoned up the front; Brittany's chocolate-brown skirt had two diagonal zippers that formed a V in the front. Jessica wore her skirt with a cream-colored silk tank, and Brittany wore hers with a flouncy chocolate-and-black geometric-patterned blouse. Jessica had been delighted to discover her new skirt matched a lit pair of lace-up booties, which made her legs look amazing. Brittany wore black platforms today—they were equally rad.

"Hey, babe."

Jessica turned and flashed her perfect white teeth at her boyfriend, Derek, a senior—the varsity football quarterback. She casually put her hand over her mouth and blew into her palm to check her breath, which was fine, of course. She lifted her cheek for a kiss.

Derek's leather letterman jacket crackled as he threw his arm around Jessica. He brushed his lips against her smooth skin. "You smell great."

She giggled and punched him in the upper arm. He flexed his muscles and grinned at her.

"Did you get your suit yet for the dance?" she asked him. She'd given him explicit instructions for the type of suit to buy—color, style, and cut; she knew what would be stellar on him. If he did as she told him, they'd look amazing together on Saturday night.

"Not yet."

Jessica leaned away from Derek and glared at him. "The dance is only three days away, Derek! You won't be able to get the suit fitted that fast. I thought you were going to get it last week!"

Derek rolled his eyes. "It's not like I've been doing nothing, Jess. Coach has us practicing more for the homecoming game, which is only two days away, you know."

Jessica stepped out from under his arm. She squinted at him. "You don't practice all the time. You could've gotten your suit."

Derek shrugged. "I'll go get something this evening."

"It won't be custom," Jessica complained. She pushed out her lips in what she knew was a pretty pout.

"Yo, Derek, Jessica!" one of their friends shouted.

Jessica turned to flutter her fingers at Chase, the school's star running back. He was trotting past, cradling his history book like a football. She watched his long, curly hair fly out behind him as he went, and then she shifted her gaze to his butt. He had a great butt, even better than Derek's. His face wasn't much—his features were too flat to be called handsome or even cute, but the butt and the curly surfer hair made up for that. Plus, he had the whole star-running-back thing going for him. This had earned him the privilege of dating Stephanie, one of the varsity cheerleaders, and Jessica's second-best friend. A *distant* second best.

The truth was that even though Jessica was friends with everyone in the school who was worth being friends with (a certain appearance and status was required to be entitled to her attentions), she'd never be as close to anyone as she was to Brittany, who was her BFF in the truest sense of the word.

Was *BFF* a word?

Jessica brushed aside the question. Who knew? Who cared?

"Gotta go, babe," Derek said. He put a rough index fingertip under her chin and lifted her face so it looked up at his.

She studied Derek's dark, handsome features. With his beautiful hair, intense brown eyes, and umber-brown skin, Derek had the kind of good looks that made Jessica's legs go weak. And, of course, Derek knew his powers every bit as much as she knew her own. He and his six feet, two inches of sculpted muscle strutted through the school's hallways like the king he was. They made an incredibly beautiful couple.

Derek gave her a soft kiss on the lips. His breath smelled like the wintergreen gum he was always chewing. She loved the smell. It went perfectly with the icy-scented cologne he wore now, which she bought for his birthday the month before. She knew he hadn't been excited about that, but he'd loved the leather steering wheel cover she'd also given him. One present he wanted. One present he needed. She knew how to be diplomatic.

Even though she loved the smell, the gum did bug her. She didn't think all that sugar was good for him.

"You're going to get cavities, you know, and all your teeth are going to, like, fall out when you get old," she always told him.

He usually ignored her. One day, though, he responded, "Yeah, and by then, we'll both be all wrinkled, and we'll have been together so long we'll probably hate each other. So, it won't matter."

She hadn't been sure what to make of that. Did that mean he planned to marry her? Did she want him to? She didn't think so.

Jessica and Brittany had plans for their future that didn't include Derek or Brittany's boyfriend, Roman, also a senior and also a football player—the star wide receiver. Admittedly, dating Derek and Roman was great for their status, and having senior boyfriends made their lives super convenient—the boys could drive them wherever they wanted to go in kick-ass convertibles without parental supervision. But that didn't mean Jessica and Brittany had met the loves of their lives. Neither of them had those illusions. Derek and Roman would likely dump them when they went off to college anyway, but that wasn't a problem. They could get new boyfriends with a snap of their fingers.

Derek started to saunter away.

Jessica caught his arm. "Derek, could you please open my locker for me?"

Derek raised a thick eyebrow but then shrugged and reached out to quickly spin her lock through the combination she knew he'd memorized. The lock clicked open, and he pulled it off. Then he yanked on the lock. It jammed, as usual. He gave it a slap with the palm of his hand, then gripped it with his index finger and thumb and jiggled it. Finally, it gave way.

"My hero," Jessica said.

Derek rolled his eyes. "Maintenance should fix that," he said.

"Like, I just said that, right?" Brittany said. She was standing in front of her own open locker, touching up her makeup in the mirror hanging on the inside of the door.

"See you at lunch, babe," Derek said to Jessica. "Bye, Brit." He strode away.

Jessica watched Brittany swirl her powder brush across her forehead. She was a whiz with makeup. She could make even the angriest of red pimples disappear with a little foundation and powder. Not that she had any acne. Like Jessica, Brittany had flawless skin. But she could make the prettiest skin look even prettier. It was a gift.

Just as Jessica started to look into her own locker, Brittany's locker door flew shut. Brittany jumped back just in time to avoid being slapped by its sharp metal edge.

"What the—?" Brittany began.

"I'm so sorry!" a chirpy voice said.

Jessica crossed her arms and attempted to skewer the owner of the voice with her best laser-like, you-are-pond-scum look. Mindy, the chirper, didn't even notice. Instead, she laughed.

She laughed.

The moron.

"Cindy and I were thumb wrestling, and my hand slipped into the door," she said, grinning. "I went out of bounds." She snorted.

So did the girl standing next to her . . . Cindy.

Jessica curled her lip and shook her head. *"Cindy and I were thumb wrestling,"* she mimicked Mindy's cartoonish voice. In her normal smooth voice, Jessica said, "Thumb wrestling?" She looked at Brittany, who was reopening her locker in a huff. When she got it open, she threw the door back so it slammed into the frame of the neighboring locker—Mindy's. It slammed so hard that it almost closed itself again. Brittany caught it.

"You two shouldn't even, like, have lockers in this section," Brittany complained. "You're eighth graders!"

Mindy smiled and shrugged. "It's not our fault the junior high school flooded."

"I'm not so sure about that," Brittany said. "You two are so stupid, you probably, like, tried to flush something down the toilet and backed up the sewer."

Jessica had to speak up. "No, Brittany," she said. "*They* are the things that should be flushed down the toilet." She shifted her attention to Mindy and her friend. "You belong in the sewers. Like little sewer rats." She lifted her hands to the sides of her nose and wiggled her fingers while she lifted her lip to expose her upper teeth. She made little squeaky sounds like a rat and looked at Mindy hard. Really hard. Any normal person on the receiving end of Jessica's flinty look would be shrinking into a little ball of shame. Jessica's dirty looks were epic.

Mindy didn't even flinch.

It annoyed Jessica to no end that neither Mindy

nor her look-alike friend, Cindy, were the least bit intimidated by Jessica or Brittany. And seriously, how too cutesy were those names? *Mindy and Cindy?* They sounded like the names of poodles or baby dolls, the kind that spoke when you pulled their cords. "Hi, my name is Mindy. Pull my cord again, and I'll burp on you."

Jessica smiled, remembering how Brittany had laughed her head off when Jessica had said this to her the week before. Brittany agreed that Cindy and Mindy were good names for dogs and dolls. They weren't good names for real girls.

They didn't look like real girls, either. Both freckled and redheaded, Mindy and Cindy were small for their thirteen years. Both were kind of cute, Jessica supposed, in a ferret or hedgehog sort of way, but she hated how Mindy's cheeks puffed out and how Cindy's eyes bulged. Not to mention their childlike clothes. The both tended to favor things like gingham and polka dots and animal prints and little floral patterns; it made them look like total babies. It was bad enough that the high school students had to put up with these *kids* in their building because of the reconstruction happening at the junior high. It was worse when those junior high kids looked and acted like grade-school kids.

Mindy tilted her head and smiled at Jessica. Jessica narrowed her eyes and lifted her chin to make it clear she was condemning Mindy to "less than" status.

Mindy didn't seem to care. "That was really cute," she said.

"What was?" Jessica asked.

Mindy lifted her hands to either side of her nose and did the same rat impression Jessica had just done.

"Are you, like, dissing her?" Brittany asked, stepping slightly in front of Jessica as if she was going to defend her physically instead of just verbally.

Mindy lifted her eyebrows. "Dissing?" She shook her head. "No, I don't diss. I think it's rude." She shrugged. "I was being serious. It was cute, what she did." She looked at Cindy. "Wasn't it, Cindy?"

Cindy nodded her head several times. Her springy curls bounced.

The curls were the way Jessica was able to tell the girls apart. Mindy's hair was straight, and it hung to just below her narrow shoulder blades.

"It was," Cindy said. "I have a gerbil at home, and she looks a lot like that when she's eating a slice of cucumber." She smiled. "Her name is Aphrodite, and she's really cute. Isn't she, Mindy?"

Mindy nodded. "She really is. See? It was a compliment, not a diss."

Brittany looked at Mindy sideways and snorted.

Cindy sneezed. And she didn't even cover her nose. Snot sprayed everywhere.

Jessica and Brittany stepped back in unison. "Get your germs away from us!" Jessica snapped.

Cindy sniffled and pulled a tissue from her pocket.

"I don't have a cold," she said. *Cold* came out *code*. "It's allergies. I'm allergic to dust."

Before Jessica could respond to that, Mindy leaned toward Brittany. "I really am sorry I accidentally slammed your locker door. I'll be more careful from now on."

"As if," Brittany said.

Mindy flashed a big smile at Brittany and Jessica. "Bye," Cindy said. "Have a good day." She sneezed again.

Jessica wrinkled her own nose.

The two eighth graders, both wearing full-skirted short dresses, hurried away. Jessica shook her head in awe. She reached into her locker and pulled a towel from her gym bag. She wiped down her arms, the front of her locker, and the front of Brittany's locker. When she was done, Brittany handed her a disinfecting wipe.

"Brilliant," Jessica said, wiping her hands. "Thanks."

"She sneezes on my locker all the time," Brittany said. "I don't care if it's allergies. It's grody."

"I know, right?" Jessica agreed.

Jessica looked down the hall and watched the little redheads go around the corner. How did they take themselves seriously? Mindy sounded like a chipmunk, with her words all clumped together and a slight *ch* attached to all her *s* sounds. But Cindy's voice was so high-pitched, she sounded like a dolphin. Even her sneezes were squeaky.

"I, like, totally hate those two," Brittany said. "They're beyond neeky."

"If uncool and neeky had a baby, it would still have more chill than those two," Jessica agreed.

Brittany laughed. She looked at the gold watch dangling from her slender white wrist. "Jess, we need to hurry. We'll be late for history."

Jessica quickly reached into her locker and grabbed her history textbook. "I'm ready," she said.

Jessica and Brittany slammed their lockers in unison and sashayed down the fast-emptying hall. They were hurrying because they both knew anyone who was late for history had to give an oral report on an assigned topic the next day, but they had to hurry without *looking* like they were hurrying. Royalty didn't hurry.

It was all about poise and grace. Jessica and Brittany had both. This was what took their looks over the top. They weren't just beautiful; they had presence. Jessica and Brittany maintained that presence at all times, even when they had to rush to class.

Jessica and Brittany made it to history with four seconds to spare, but now they were sweeping into the school cafeteria ten minutes late. The huge room was packed; the buzz of animated conversations nearly drowned out pop music playing from speakers overhead. It looked like the long metal tables were full, but Jessica knew space would magically appear when she and Brittany were ready to sit down. It was sort of like

Moses and that sea . . . what was the name of it? Whatever. It was the way Moses made the water stand up
and get out of the way. Jessica and Brittany had similar powers.

All they had to do was walk through the crowd, and
kids would stand up and make space for them. Even
before they officially were named queen and princess,
they'd had regal powers.

Both Jessica's and Brittany's moms were cheerleaders and homecoming and prom queens when they
were in high school, this very school . . . before it got
infected with junior high kids. They went on to be
cheerleaders and queens in college, too. Jessica's mom
was runner-up in a national pageant as well. Brittany's
mom was a runway model before she married
Brittany's dad. It seemed Jessica's and Brittany's noble
status was in their DNA.

"Did you, like, put some of those berries we got at
the farmers market in your smoothie?" Brittany asked
Jessica as they started walking toward the heart of the
huge beige-walled room stuffed with long tables,
snarfing kids, and food smells that made their noses
wrinkle. Jessica's nose told her the entrée of the day
was fish sticks, and the side dish was brussels sprouts
and cabbage. Who ate that?

"As if I'd forget," Jessica said. She elbowed her friend
and gave her a pretend dirty look.

Brittany laughed. "I hope they smell as sweet as
they did when we got them. Like, that, um, stinky

cabbage is going to ruin my nose forever. It's beyond disgusting."

"I know, right?"

They kept walking through the throng, totally unconcerned about finding a place to sit. And yes, there it was.

Jessica smiled when she saw a couple boys from their English class stand up and vacate their seats as Jessica and Brittany approached. "You can sit here," one of them, Evan, said as he stepped away from the table. He was kind of cute in a hobo-vibe sort of way. His clothes were always hanging off him, and they were all retro. But he had great hooded eyes and a fluid way of moving that kept him from being a dweeb.

Jessica turned up the amps on her smile and aimed for the vacated space as Evan and his friend walked away. Before she could get to it, though, both of the folding beige metal chairs were taken . . . by Mindy and Cindy.

The two girls darted in from the opposite direction, plopped down, and immediately pulled sandwiches from little-kid lunch boxes. Cindy's had flowers on it; Mindy's had a pink unicorn on the side.

"Are you, like, kidding me?" Brittany asked. She stood shoulder-to-shoulder with Jessica and stared at the two upstarts. "Just, like, who do they think they are, right?"

Although the vast majority of the kids in the cafeteria were unaware of the colossal faux pas that had just been made, everyone at the table Evan and his friend had just vacated went silent. All the occupants at the two adjoining tables stopped talking, too. Every kid at the silenced tables craned their necks to stare at the two redheaded girls. That made thirty-one pairs of eyes that shifted from the oblivious girls at the table to the dumbfounded girls hovering behind them.

Jessica ground her teeth . . . for half a second. Then she remembered that grinding her teeth was bad for them. She set her shoulders and raised her chin. "Excuse me," she said evenly. Her tone was as placid as a lake on a calm day, but it was just as benign as the jagged-toothed eels that lurked below the lake's surface. She'd been bitten by an eel like that when she was a little girl. She knew how surface appearances could be deceiving, and she delighted in being that placid lake in situations like these. It was so much fun to bring out the eels once you got others to relax and think all was well.

Mindy, her pudgy cheeks puffed out even more than usual by whatever food she had stuffed in her mouth, looked up at Jessica. "Oh, hi." She looked back down at the peanut butter and jelly sandwich lying on plastic wrap in front of her.

"Do you really think 'Oh, hi' is the appropriate response when someone says, 'Excuse me'?" Jessica asked Mindy.

Cindy looked up from what smelled like a tuna sandwich. She glanced around at all the kids at the table. Her bug-like hazel eyes blinked several times. "What's the matter?" she asked. "Did we break some rule?" She sniffled and pulled out a tissue to wipe her nose.

"Seriously, like what classes do you two take?" Brittany asked. "Eighth-Grade Oblivious? Junior-Level Rude?"

Jessica chuckled. She loved her friend's sense of humor.

Mindy frowned and put down her sandwich. "I don't get what's going on."

"That's, like, duh, exactly my point," Brittany said.

Jessica pointed at the two seats Mindy and Cindy occupied. "Those are our seats."

Mindy raised an eyebrow. "They are?" She turned and looked behind her seat back. "I don't see names. Did we get assigned seating?"

Jessica widened her eyes. "Are you for real?"

The girl sitting next to Cindy, a junior-varsity cheerleader named Valerie—a girl Jessica thought had a lot of potential—leaned over and whispered to Cindy.

Cindy screwed up her face, whether in confusion or concentration wasn't clear. When Valerie leaned back, Cindy said in her ear-piercing squeak, "Really?"

Mindy looked at her. "What?"

Cindy pointed at Valerie. "She says that these seats were being saved for Jessica and Brittany." She sneezed and then blew into her tissue.

Mindy glanced up and looked around the table. She zeroed in on the one empty place on the end. She stood and looked around. Spotting a single empty seat at one of the other tables filled with kids paused mid-lunch, still quietly watching the unfolding drama, Mindy strode over and grabbed the metal chair. Dragging it back across the linoleum floor with an annoying metallic scrape, she positioned it next to the single seat at the end of the table. She looked at Cindy. "Can you grab my lunch, please, Cindy? You and I can squeeze in here. There's enough space as long as we don't try to chair dance while we eat." She laughed and plopped in the chair she'd stolen from the other table.

"Sure," Cindy said. She sniffled, then gathered both hers and Mindy's lunch boxes. She stood and carried them to the small open place at the table next to Mindy.

Jessica tapped her foot as she watched the girls' audacious behavior. She glanced at Brittany, who was opening and closing her mouth as if she was trying to remember how to talk. For several more seconds, Jessica looked from the now-vacant chairs to the silly girls at the end of the table. They weren't paying any attention to Jessica or Brittany. They were leaning toward each other, chattering away as if nothing had happened.

Jessica sighed and sat down. Brittany settled in next to her.

Jessica shrugged, and said, "Eighth graders. You can't live with them, and you can't, like . . . kill them."

Everyone laughed and returned to their lunches.

Jessica shook her head and unscrewed the lid of her sleek silver insulated cup. It contained the fruit smoothie she always drank midday. It wasn't like her complexion took no work at all, right? She had to take some precautions against breakouts. Consuming the right combination of fruits and supplements was a must.

Brittany agreed with Jessica about that, but usually she drank her smoothie in the morning. For lunch, she liked having a cup of vegetable soup, which her family's cook prepared and placed in a thermal mug and tucked inside a small cotton-canvas-and-rattan tote. It was a stylish carrier, in a save-the-planet-chic kind of way.

Brittany pulled out her thermal mug and peered into the tote. "OMG, Frieda." She sighed.

"She, like, forgot your spoon again, right?" Jessica said.

"She so forgot my spoon!" Brittany looked around as if she could summon Frieda from home to remedy the unforgivable error.

Jessica clicked her tongue, then looked down the table at Mindy. "Mindy!" She said the girl's name the same way she said her dog Titan's name when he tried to dig in her ficus tree planter at home. The tone was sharp enough to compensate for the fact that it wasn't very loud.

Mindy's head shot up. She was chewing again, her round cheeks bobbing up and down in a counter rhythm to her dimpled chin. She looked at Jessica and pointed at herself.

Jessica rolled her eyes. "No, the other Mindy?"

Mindy looked around the table, as if searching for the other Mindy.

"OMG," Brittany said again. This time, Jessica knew she was referencing Mindy's complete ignorance.

"Yes, you." Jessica nodded at Mindy. "Could you please get my friend here a spoon? Since you delayed our lunch, right? It seems, like, the least you can do."

"It is, right?" Brittany agreed.

Mindy swallowed what was in her mouth and shrugged. "Sure." She popped up. "Just a second." She trotted off.

Jessica leaned toward Brittany. "Maybe we could train them to be like those, what were they called? The maids that helped royal women get dressed?"

"Ladies-in-waiting, right?" Brittany said.

"That's it, totally."

Mindy handed Brittany the spoon and returned to her seat. She went right back to her little-kid sandwich as if she hadn't just been ordered around. Jessica smiled and imagined Mindy and Cindy scurrying behind her and Brittany wherever they went. It was a seriously sick image.

The rest of lunch passed without incident until Mindy and Cindy got up from the table just seconds after Jessica and Brittany did. All four girls headed to the cafeteria exit.

Because Jessica and Brittany had arrived late to lunch and had taken their time, most of the cafeteria had cleared out by the time they got ready to leave.

"Are they, like, following us?" Brittany asked Jessica, gesturing over her shoulder with her chin.

Jessica shook her head. "I think they're too spacey to even know they're behind us." She could hear the eighth graders babbling away behind her. They were discussing something about getting a ride from their moms.

"Hey, babe!" Derek called from a couple tables away. "Hey, Brit!"

Next to him, Roman shot a finger at Brittany, then winked at her. He saluted Jessica.

Jessica and Brittany stopped to pose for their boyfriends. They did it as a matter of course. It was just what came naturally when the boys were looking at them.

"Burgers after practice?" Derek called.

Jessica and Brittany nodded and blew the guys a kiss.

Then they turned and glided toward the cafeteria exit. It was always important to leave while you still had them hanging on.

At the exit, Brittany suddenly lurched to a stop and almost fell over. Jessica grabbed her friend's arm and kept her from going down. She also immediately saw why Brittany had almost fallen flat on her face.

Mindy was kneeling right in the middle of the exit, tying the rainbow-colored shoelaces on her sparkling purple shoes. As she tied, she babbled at Cindy, who stood next to her. "Mom said we can stay at the dance until eleven! I'm so jazzed. I had my dress out last night. The ruffles are so pretty!"

"Can you even believe that?" Jessica asked no one in particular.

Mindy popped up. "Believe what?" She looked from Jessica to Brittany, who was attempting to slice Mindy to bits with her icy look. "What? Oh, oops. I was in the way, wasn't I?"

"Ding, ding, ding," Jessica sang.

"Huh?" Mindy said.

Cindy, who had been a few feet from her friend, turned back. "What's going on?"

Mindy shook her head. "I was being thoughtless." She smiled up at the older girls. "I really am sorry, guys." She turned to walk away.

Jessica grabbed Mindy's arm and yanked her out of the doorway.

"Hey," Cindy objected. Then she sneezed. She glared furiously at Jessica as she dug out a tissue.

Mindy didn't say anything. She let Jessica pull her off to the side of the last few stragglers coming out of the cafeteria. Cindy immediately rushed to Mindy's side.

Jessica let go of Mindy's pudgy baby arm. "Tell me you were not talking about the homecoming dance just now. Because you *couldn't* have been talking about that dance."

Mindy grinned. "Sure, I was talking about the homecoming dance. Everyone's talking about it. You're going to look really pretty with the crown on. I'm sure of it. What color will your dress be?"

Jessica opened her mouth, then closed it. She turned toward Brittany. "Since when do eighth graders come to the high school dances?"

Before Brittany could answer, one of their fellow

cheerleaders, Patrice, brushed past. "Oh, don't get me started, you know? You didn't hear that the principal said that as long as they're in classes here, they should be included in the dances?"

Patrice flipped her shiny black hair and made a face. "It's insanity." She shrugged and strode away.

Jessica turned back to Mindy. She made a face when she got a whiff of Mindy's peanut-butter breath. "You do know that you're *nobody*, right?"

The pale skin between Mindy's reddish-blonde brows furrowed. "Is that slang for something?"

Brittany snorted.

Jessica shook her head. "No, you poor pitiful thing. It's fact. You're nobody. You and your bug-eyed friend. You. Are. Nobody. You're coming to the dance together? Because no one asked you out, right? Who would, right?"

"For sure," Brittany said.

Mindy's face flushed. Jessica waited for the tears to start.

But they didn't come.

Instead, Mindy shook her head and smiled. "I feel really sorry for you."

"What?!" Jessica gawked at Mindy.

"Really," Mindy said. "I'm sorry. You must not like yourself very much."

"What?!" This time Brittany joined in with her friend. Brittany's *what* was even higher pitched than Jessica's.

Mindy nodded. She turned to Cindy. "Remember what our moms said, Cindy?"

Cindy bobbed her head and sent her curls shaking. "Sure. When kids are mean to you, it's because they really want to be mean to themselves, but they can't. They're . . . I think Mom said *projecting*." She sniffed, then blew her nose.

"That sounds right," Mindy agreed. She looked up at Jessica. "It's okay. You can't help it. If it makes you feel better to be mean to us, go ahead."

"No one likes you!" Jessica practically screamed.

Mindy looked around at a couple dozen kids who had stopped to watch what was going on. She chewed on her lower lip. Then she shrugged. "Well, I don't know if that's true. But if it is, that's okay, too. Because *we* like us, don't we, Cindy?"

Cindy nodded. "We sure do." Clutching her snot-filled tissue, she put her arm around Mindy. "We're friends forever. We do everything together."

Mindy nodded. "That's enough for us." She glanced up at the clock above the cafeteria door. "Sorry to be rude, but we need to get to robotics class."

Mindy and Cindy turned and hurried away. Jessica stared after them, her mouth hanging open. She felt Brittany take her arm. "Come on, Jess. We need to get to robotics class, too."

Jessica made a sound not unlike the one Titan made when he spotted a squirrel in his backyard. It was a cross between a growl and a groan.

"I don't know if I can, like, look at those two for the next hour," she whispered to Brittany.

"I know, right? Can you even believe what she said? It was, like, cray-cray."

Jessica didn't respond. She was too angry.

Projecting, she thought. *The nerve of the little—*

"Come on," Brittany said. "We'll figure out what to do about them later. We don't want to miss robotics. Remember? Mr. Thornton is assigning our projects today. I don't want something too difficult."

Jessica sighed. "Good point. Let's go."

The robotics classroom was in a mostly deserted wing of the school. Jessica knew the wing still had storage rooms that were accessed from time to time, but the classroom that robotics was in was the only one being used. The school once had a very active art program and dance program in this wing, but budget cuts had shut down those curricula. Money was funneled into robotics and computer programming instead of the arts, and even that wasn't enough money. The reason their class was using old, donated animatronics was because there were no funds to buy state-of-the-art robotic parts. The classroom didn't get much attention from janitorial or maintenance, either. It was usually far too dusty to suit Jessica.

But Jessica didn't care either way about the arts or robotics. She wasn't particularly good at computers, painting, or dance. Her forte was form, not function.

Oh, and that reminded her—maintenance should do something about the *function* of her locker.

The robotics classroom was a large warehouse-like room with tall ceilings guarded by exposed metal beams. The floors were covered with rubberized interlocking squares, and the metal worktables were bright red. Gray pegboards lined the walls of the room, and every robotics part you could think of hung on hooks from those boards. The room was far too industrial to suit Jessica's tastes, but she tolerated it like everyone else.

Even though robotics was a required class for sophomores, and many of Jessica's classmates groused about it, she secretly didn't mind it. Most of the time she didn't really understand what she was doing, but she did think it was fun. And it played into her other strength: control. Of course, she liked control best when she was controlling *people*, but controlling machines seemed to be a natural extension of that.

Even with all her beauty and social skills, Jessica never got everything and everyone around her to act just as she wanted them to. There was always someone who was saying the wrong thing or doing the wrong thing. Take the two redheaded morons, for instance. With her class popularity and physical presence, she should have been able to wrap Mindy and Cindy around her manicured finger. That they didn't afford her the appropriate amount of reverence was like having a splinter stuck just under the skin. She hated when that happened. She hated Mindy and Cindy even more.

The room's red tables sat in rows, three tables in each of the five rows. Jessica and Brittany took their seats at the middle table in the third row—not too close to the front so they wouldn't appear to be geeks, not too close to the back where they'd be surrounded by outcasts. They always sat where their vaulted status could be recognized.

The robotics teacher, Mr. Thornton, a short twentysomething man with birdlike features—beady eyes, a pointed nose, and fine brown hair—strode into the class and set a stack of books and schematics on his desk. Jessica shook her head at the red-and-gold diamond-patterned sweater vest that hung loosely over Mr. Thornton's narrow chest. Between the vests he always wore and his thick, black-rimmed glasses, Mr. Thornton was the poster boy for geeks everywhere.

Mr. Thornton looked askance at the class, as he always did. He had a little trouble with eye contact. He never faced straight at the class, and when you talked to him directly, he focused his gaze about a foot above your head. Jessica thought that was sort of endearing, in a lovable-nerd kind of way.

"Talk among yourselves for a few minutes. The shipment just came in, and I need to supervise the . . ." He trailed off and disappeared into the workroom adjacent to the robotics classroom.

That was something else Mr. Thornton did. He frequently left his sentences unfinished. It was weird.

Once, Brittany suggested that Mr. Thornton might be an animatronic, one with advanced programming and a minor glitch that prevented him from completing his communications. Jessica thought that was hysterically funny.

"What do you want to do about them?" Brittany asked.

Jessica blinked and looked at her friend. "What? About who?"

Brittany nodded toward Mindy and Cindy, who were sitting in the front row. Jessica looked at the backs of the two redheads.

Mindy and Cindy had only joined the class a couple weeks before. Apparently, they were part of some gifted class that did robotics competitions. They even worked out of the robotics lab—meeting early each morning before the school day began. And now they were auditing the sophomore class. Little freaks.

Jessica opened her mouth to answer her friend, but before she could, a loud clattering and thumping accompanied Mr. Thornton back into the room. The racket came from the wheels of a cart he was pushing in front of him. The cart was piled with things that looked like they should have been either in old sci-fi movies, amusement parks, or circuses.

Momentarily forgetting Mindy and Cindy, Jessica sat up straight and leaned forward to see what was on the cart. She spotted a couple of silver robot skeletons, vaguely man-shaped gray robots that looked like aliens, and several mechanical animals. Many were dog- and cat-shaped, and a few looked like miniature barn animals and exotic animals. She spotted a cow, a horse, an orangutan, a black panther, a flamingo, and a huge pink pig. The pig was the only life-sized thing on the cart. The cow, horse, and panther were about the same size as the dogs and cats.

All the mechanical animals looked like they were designed to stand on their back two feet, and most wore some piece of clothing or accessory, reminding her more of sports team mascots than real animals. Jessica saw a couple bow ties and vests, two feather boas, short pants with suspenders (on the flamingo), a bowler hat, striped socks, and a pair of red gloves. The pig was the closest to being fully dressed; it wore what looked like a frilly waitress uniform in a shade of pink just a little darker than its fuzzy piggy skin. Atop its broad head sat a pillbox-shaped pink cap with a ruffled edge. Other than the outfit, and the fact that it had fuzzy pink hands instead of hooves, it looked a lot like a real pig.

"Okay, class, let's get started on today's . . ." Mr. Thornton said. He gestured at the cartload of robotic characters he'd just dragged in and grinned sideways at the class. "What we have here is a vintage animatronic bonanza!" He uttered one of his rare laughs.

Jessica winced. She was glad his laughs were rare; he sounded like a tortured mouse when he laughed.

Mr. Thornton sobered. "None of these animatronics function at the moment, but every one of them is capable of . . . You'll partner up, and each partnership will get one of these to work on, so it will be . . . You'll have two jobs to do. First, do whatever is needed so your animatronic will function as it's supposed to, and second, program it so it performs some specific task. You will then either have it perform for the class or videotape it if the function is done outside of class where we can't . . . Each one of these has something to teach us, so let's . . ."

He moved over to the cart and pulled out one of the small dog robots. It wore a yellow dog sweater.

"This dog is an example of an animatronic that uses servos, and we all know that servos are controlled by . . ." Mr. Thornton looked out over the top of the class and pushed his glasses up onto his nose. "Anyone?"

Mindy raised her hand. "Servos are controlled by sending an electrical pulse through the control wire."

"Good," Mr. Thornton said.

Jessica rolled her eyes.

"When a servo goes bad," Mr. Thornton continued, "it's usually because of one of seven problems we discussed yesterday. Does anyone want to give us a review of . . ."

He pointed at Cindy when her hand shot up. "Contamination, like from oil or coolant; bad bearings; electrical degradation; poor installation, like the belts are too tight or couplings are worn out; a bad power supply or drive; damaged cables; or overload."

"Good," Mr. Thornton said. "So, this dog"—he set

the animatronic dog on his desk—"has a bad servo. Cindy, you and Mindy can take this."

Cindy and Mindy clapped their hands like five-year-olds. Mr. Thornton grinned at a spot above their heads and set the dog on the table in front of them.

Mr. Thornton turned to the cart and grabbed the orangutan, a goat, and a cat. "More servo issues with these. Let's see who . . ."

Mr. Thornton parceled out the robotic animals.

Brittany leaned close to Jessica and whispered, "Do we want to work on a servo problem?"

Jessica shrugged. "Whatever."

Mr. Thornton returned to the front of the class after handing out several of the mechanical animals. "Although servos have a lot of pros in terms of their functionality," Mr. Thornton said, stopping by the cart, "there can be noise issues with . . ." He reached out and grabbed the animatronic flamingo. He activated it, and when it moved its legs, the mechanism screeched. Mr. Thornton turned it off. "Pneumatic setups, by comparison, are fairly quiet and . . ." He got up and approached the cart.

Wrestling with the exoskeletons and human-shaped animatronics, Mr. Thornton unburied the pig at the bottom of what was left of the pile. Now that it was lying on its back on the cart, alone, Jessica could clearly see the pig's pink potbelly, stubby legs, and sweetly smiling face. The mechanical pig was old; Jessica could see glinting silver showing through the pig's pink felt layer here and there.

Mr. Thornton gestured at the prone pig. "Meet Rosie Porkchop. Rosie has a pneumatic system, which means she can lift a lot more weight than her fellow . . . She has a lot of pressure pumping through her lines, so she has quite a bit of potential, but her programming is . . . Obviously, she's too heavy to move, except on this cart. Whoever gets her will have to come back in the evenings to work on her, so . . ."

Jessica nudged Brittany and hissed, "Don't look at him."

They'd already had to do one after-hours project this year, and she didn't want to—

"Jessica and Brittany, you two get Rosie."

Jessica and Brittany groaned in unison.

"Now let's get the rest of these passed . . . ," Mr. Thornton said.

Brittany whispered to Jessica. "Seriously? We have to come back here this evening and work on a pig?"

Jessica rolled her eyes. Maybe she *didn't* like robotics class after all.

When Jessica and Brittany returned to the robotics classroom after cheerleading practice, freshly showered and once again wearing their school outfits, they found Mr. Thornton at his desk and Rosie, on the cart by herself, at the back of the room.

Mr. Thornton looked up and gazed just past Jessica's shoulder. "There you are. I put Rosie at the back for you to work . . . Sorry she's too big to remove from the school, but . . . I had to assign her to a team I could trust to stay after-hours so I could get administrative approval for you to be in here for . . ." He waved a hand toward Rosie. "She's all yours."

Jessica and Brittany exchanged a glance, sighed in unison, and went to the back of the class. Together, they set down their leather backpacks. Jessica reached into hers, grabbed her lip gloss, and touched up her lips. Brittany did the same.

They stood together and looked at the pig.

"Uh, girls?" Mr. Thornton called out.

They turned. He waved a thin stack of papers at them. "Here are some specs that came with Rosie when she . . . You'll want to take a look at them. She's not your typical animatronic, and she has a characteristic that it's important for you . . ."

Jessica strode over and took the papers. "We'll read everything, like, super carefully," she said.

Mr. Thornton nodded. "I'll be here for a little while longer if you have any questions for . . ."

"Thanks, Mr. Thornton."

Jessica returned to Brittany and dropped the papers on the table next to Rosie. Neither girl looked at them. They returned to looking at the pig.

"It's so, like, big," Brittany said. She sighed.

Jessica nodded. She glared at the huge pig.

The sound of dual giggles suddenly burst into the room behind Jessica and Brittany. They turned and watched Cindy and Mindy skip over to Mr. Thornton.

Mindy carried the dog animatronic they were working on.

"Why did they get, like, a small one?" Brittany asked.

Jessica shook her head. She watched the little brats chatter with Mr. Thornton. Then she turned and looked at Rosie. She looked back at the brats and then back to Rosie.

She grinned and nudged Brittany.

"Picture this," Jessica whispered. She held her hands out in front of her like she was framing a screen. "Little Mindy and Cindy"—she jerked her head to indicate the two girls who were still talking with the teacher— "are walking into the homecoming dance, like they're all that. They're like, 'We don't care if anyone likes us. We like *ourselves*.'" In a continued whisper, she mimicked Mindy's chipmunk voice.

Brittany made a face and nodded.

"And along comes our new BFF Rosie Porkchop, large and in charge." Jessica held out her arms to indicate the animatronic pig's size. "She's been programmed, by us, of course, to walk right up to those two little twerps, knock them down, and . . . "—she grinned—" sit on them."

Brittany laughed loudly, and Jessica shushed her. Brittany covered her mouth, then hugged Jessica. "That's brilliant!" she whispered. "Is that the task we'll give her, like, for our project?"

Jessica rolled her eyes. "We should probably have her

do something that won't get us in trouble, don't you think?"

Brittany blushed and nodded.

"But this might be more fun than I thought it was going to be," Jessica said.

"For sure," Brittany agreed.

Jessica opened her backpack and pulled out her laptop. "I don't think this should take very long. We just need to download her command software and go over it until we find her glitch, and then we can tweak it to do what we want her to do."

Brittany nodded but frowned. "Um, you do know, like, we suck at programming, right?"

Jessica shrugged. "Yeah, but that'll give us a nice alibi later. We can say we have no idea what went wrong with the programming, what made Rosie go crazy and knock them over or spill punch on them or whatever. And besides, it's the complicated programming stuff we always get wrong. This is just basic programming of voice commands, right?"

She pulled up a seat and placed it next to Rosie's front end. Sitting with her legs perfectly crossed, Jessica lifted the flap that hid Rosie's controls. "First, we just need to create the uplink, and then . . ." She pressed a button.

A soft *puff*, followed by a series of metallic clicks and snaps that preceded a louder *whoosh*, and both girls jumped when Rosie's lower belly popped open.

"What did you do?" Brittany asked. "Is she going to, like, have babies?"

Jessica laughed, but then she shrugged. What if there were animatronic piglets inside Rosie? Even with the mechanisms that she must have had inside her exo-skeleton, Rosie certainly was big enough to store at least a dozen of them, if not more.

After exchanging a glance, Jessica and Brittany both bent over to peer into Rosie's belly.

Expecting to see a full system of hydraulics—and possibly a few baby pigs, Jessica raised her eyebrow when she saw that Rosie's belly was, for the most part, empty. A network of metal gears, prongs, and sharp-looking rods—presumably powered by hydraulics—lined the interior wall of the pig's belly, but the vast majority of the cavernous space was totally open . . . and big enough to hold a person, maybe two at most.

Jessica stared into Rosie Porkchop's depths. She grinned and leaned back.

Glancing up at Mr. Thornton, who was still focused on his laptop, Jessica tugged on Brittany's hand. Brittany turned to look at Jessica.

"I have an even better idea than my original one," Jessica whispered.

"What?" Brittany whispered back.

Jessica hummed as she picked up the papers Mr. Thornton had handed her and began to skim through them. Brittany looked over her shoulder.

Flipping pages, Jessica reached a section titled "General Operation." Under that was a paragraph in bold:

ROSIE PORKCHOP IS A DUAL-PURPOSE ANIMATRONIC.
THE SYSTEM CAN BE ENGAGED IN TRADITIONAL ANI-
MATRONIC MODE AND ALSO IN HUMAN INTERFACE OR
"SUIT" MODE, I.E., ROSIE CAN BE "WORN" LIKE A SUIT.

There was more, but Jessica's gaze flicked down the page to the word WARNING, which was followed by a paragraph of bold red writing. Jessica quickly read through it:

ROSIE PORKCHOP CONTAINS SPRINGLOCKS. SPRINGLOCKS ENGAGE TO ALLOW ROSIE PORKCHOP TO FUNCTION AUTONOMOUSLY, IN ANIMATRONIC MODE. WHEN ENGAGED, METAL COMPONENTS FILL THE ENTIRE INTERIOR OF THE ANIMATRONIC. ROSIE PORKCHOP CAN ALSO BE WORN AS A SUIT; THIS IS CALLED HUMAN INTERFACE MODE. WHEN ROSIE PORKCHOP IS IN HUMAN INTERFACE MODE, THE SPRINGLOCKS DISENGAGE AND RETRACT INTO ROSIE'S ENDOSKELETON. DO NOT SWITCH MODES WHILE ROSIE PORKCHOP IS OCCUPIED. SHARP COMPONENTS OF THE SPRINGLOCK SYSTEM CAN CAUSE SERIOUS BODILY HARM.

She grinned and looked at Brittany. "Guess what?"
"What?"
"Rosie can be occupied."
"So?"
Jessica didn't answer. She quickly glanced through Rosie's upload instructions.

While she did that, Cindy and Mindy called out, "Bye, Mr. Thornton."

Jessica and Brittany turned to watch the little redheads skip out of the classroom. Jessica glanced at Mr. Thornton; his gaze was on his laptop.

Jessica dropped the papers, grabbed Brittany's hand, and pulled her close. She whispered, "So forget what I said before. I have a better idea."

"What?"

Jessica glanced again at Mr. Thornton. He was still concentrating on his computer. Even so, she turned her back and kept her voice low. "Rosie's pneumatic system powers that trapdoor, and it's designed to be a hermetic seal."

Brittany frowned a question.

"You know, those seals that keep in anything."

"Oh, right."

"The instructions said something about using Rosie as a container for something." She waved a hand. "I don't know. I didn't read it closely. But here's what I'm thinking." She scooted her chair closer to Brittany's. "Those two little snots think they can come to the homecoming dance. Well, they're coming all right, but not in their ruffled little dresses. They're coming in her." She pointed at Rosie Porkchop, specifically at Rosie's gaping belly.

Brittany looked at Rosie's empty stomach and slowly started to grin. "We're going to stick them in there?"

Jessica shook her head. "We aren't. We'll have Rosie

do it. It will serve them right. They'll be all like, 'We do everything together,' from inside Rosie Porkchop!"

"Oh, that's, like, inspired!" Brittany said.

"I know, right?"

Brittany nodded, her eyes bright. "This is going to be so savage!"

Jessica grinned. "All we have to do is program Rosie to grab the little snots and put them into her belly. Once they're in, this door will close." She pointed to the pink door that hung open under Rosie's belly. She tapped it. "See? It has the soft sealed fabric stuff on the outside, but it's hard metal on the inside. Once it's locked and sealed, they won't be able to get out." She grinned. "They'll be trapped together."

Brittany nodded again. "I love it."

Jessica smiled. "Good. Me too." She sighed. "There's just one problem."

"What?"

"It's going to take us a while." Jessica reached into Rosie's control panel and pulled out a clump of wires. "How about I just get the uplink going and then we can go have burgers with the guys? After that, we'll come back here and spend the evening programming Rosie."

"Okay."

Jessica opened her laptop and connected the upload wire. She handed another wire to Brittany. "Plug that into the wall. I guess she has to charge, too."

Brittany nodded and dutifully plugged in the pig. Then she watched Jessica create an uplink with Rosie.

Jessica noticed Brittany examining her nails again, then saw her friend stand to get her backpack.

Brittany snapped her fingers and sat back down.

"What?" Jessica asked.

"When I reached for my backpack, I had an idea. Instead of just"—she lowered her voice to a whisper—"trapping them, why don't we program Rosie to serve us while they're stuck inside? That will make Mindy and Cindy like our own ladies' maid. They can be our servant, like, fetching things for us and waiting on us."

"Like royalty," Jessica said, beaming. "You're so good!"

Brittany took a bow. She looked at Mr. Thornton, who had stood up at his desk. "Hurry up and get everything going. I can't wait to do this!"

"Me neither!" Jessica grinned and returned to her task. This was why she loved Brittany so much. She and Jessica had, like, shared thoughts. They always agreed, and one of them nearly always could take the other's idea and make it better. They made an unstoppable team.

Jessica tapped a couple keys and got the upload started. Then she grabbed her backpack and headed toward the door. Brittany followed her.

Because robotics was in the mostly deserted wing that could be locked off from the rest of the school, Mr. Thornton had gotten permission from the principal to let some of his students come in after-hours to work on projects. They used an exterior door that gave them access to this wing only.

Before they reached the door, Jessica called out, "Mr. Thornton."

"Hmm?" He didn't look up from his computer.

"We've got Rosie's upload going. We're going to come back later to work on her. Can we have the after-hours key?"

"Sounds good. Hmm? Oh, sure. Yes." Mr. Thornton pulled a key from his desk drawer.

Jessica took the key from their teacher, and the girls headed to the classroom door. "Bye, Mr. Thornton," they called in unison as they left.

"Oh, good-bye," he called after them.

As they walked away, Brittany said, "He said 'good-bye,' not 'bye.'"

Jessica glanced at her friend. "So?"

"Hmm? Oh, I don't know. I guess it just sounds, like, kinda final, you know?"

Jessica grinned and hugged Brittany. "You slay me!"

Jessica and Brittany, on Derek's and Roman's arms, crossed the crowded parking lot in front of Burgerdom, a local fast-food hangout known for the best burgers in the county and even better milkshakes. If it wasn't for the food, Jessica wouldn't have been caught dead in the place—it was housed in a bright orange building shaped like a hamburger bun. How cliché could you get? But it was the in place to be after school.

The parking lot was filled with cars, bicycles, and big groups of students on foot. At least three different radios played, creating a musical war between rap, pop, and country. A few junior girls were dancing at the edge of the lot. Jessica recognized most of her classmates among the crowd, and many of them were watching the royal couples head toward the restaurant's lobby. Because the pavement was uneven, Jessica shifted her gaze to her feet. She wasn't about to trip and put a hitch in her perfect glide.

Her downcast attention, however, didn't warn her of other potential hazards.

Suddenly, a bicycle swept past Jessica, its back wheels barely missing her left toes. She faltered, and if it hadn't been for Derek's arm, which she quickly clutched with all her strength, she would have lost her balance.

"Watch where you're going!" Derek bellowed at the bicyclist.

Jessica looked up to see who had nearly run over her toes, and she sighed dramatically.

"Of course," she muttered.

"What, babe?" Derek asked.

Jessica smiled up at him. She didn't want to get into it, so she just said, "Eighth graders."

"Yeah. Tell me about it. They're everywhere."

Jessica glanced at Brittany, who gave Jessica a quick smile. She'd also noticed that the kid on the bike had been Mindy. Jessica was sure Brittany was thinking the same thing: It wouldn't be long before they got payback.

"Oh man," Derek said as he pushed open

Burgerdom's double glass doors. "Look at the line. This is worse than Friday nights after a game."

Jessica noted the semi-line-shaped cluster of students pressing into the lobby, waiting their turn to order. Inhaling the smells of onions, french fries, and char-broiled burgers, she scanned the tables in the small dining area. Every one of the orange-topped metal tables was occupied. Every dark blue booth was jammed with kids. And half of them, she couldn't help but notice, were munchkins, clearly seventh and eighth graders.

"It's bad enough they're in our school," she said, "but now they're taking over our hangouts, too?"

"I know, right?" Brittany said.

It was amazing that Brittany had even heard Jessica. The noise level in the place was more rock concert than restaurant. Jessica threw back her hair and lifted her chin.

"Excuse me," she said loud enough to prompt the kids in front of her to turn. She stepped toward them. "You need to let me by." She said it in the same tone her mother used for everyone who worked for her. It was a cross between imperious and soothing, just the right combination to make a person feel like not only was it impossible for them to say no but they'd feel better after saying yes.

The kids parted, and Jessica swept through the opening. When she reached the next barrier of kids, she repeated the process. In under twenty seconds, she stood at the shiny silver counter in front of a kitchen filled with scurrying orange-and-blue-clad losers who were too poor or too ugly to get a decent job. More such losers stood behind two cash registers. One of those wore a nametag that read, IRWIN.

Irwin was ringing up an order, but he glanced over at Jessica and grinned at her.

"Hey, Irwin," she said in a tone that suggested she couldn't possibly be happier to see anyone. "You're rocking the orange and blue today!"

Irwin, a skinny guy with bad skin and worse teeth, flushed. "Hi, Jessica," he said as he counted out change to the threesome in front of his register.

As soon as Irwin closed his register and the three kids clutching an orange #17 started to move aside, Jessica stepped in front of the next kids in line. "Could you get us our usual, Irwin?" She turned and gestured toward Derek, Brittany, and Roman, who hadn't yet made it through the throng. Jessica secretly reveled in her superior crowd-parting skills. Brittany was pretty good at getting a room to do her bidding, but she couldn't compete with Jessica.

Irwin glanced around and frowned. "Um . . . ," he began.

"I know they were next." Jessica gestured at the kids breathing on her neck . . . like, literally. One of the girls was chewing grape gum, and not only was her hot breath on Jessica's skin, the grape smell was strong enough to dominate the grill smells. "But we are in such a rush, with, like, homecoming duties and such. If you could just . . ." She flipped her hair and locked her blue eyes on Irwin's pale brown ones.

He shrugged and tapped in the order.

One of the boys behind Jessica protested, "Dude."

Irwin tried to reassure him. "This'll just take a second."

Grape-gum girl, a volleyball player whose name Jessica couldn't remember—she didn't have to remember it; the girl wasn't anyone worth bothering about—sighed loudly, exhaling spitty gum breath into Jessica's hair. She'd have to go home and shower before she and Brittany went back to the school to start programming Rosie Porkchop.

"Thanks so much, Irwin," Jessica said. She took money from her backpack and paid for the food. She knew Derek would reimburse her immediately. He never wanted her to pay for anything. *That's the guy's job*, he always said. It was so sweet.

Irwin took her money, gave her change, and handed her an orange plastic #18. She flashed him a smile designed to leave him feeling like he was special, even though he clearly wasn't; then she turned.

Grape-gum girl gave Jessica a dirty look.

Jessica leaned close to her ear. "Get over it. And you might want to invest in some tweezers. Your eyebrows are growing together."

Jessica walked away and didn't care even a little that grape-gum girl was glaring at her back. Jessica could feel it, but it so didn't matter.

When Jessica returned to Brittany, Derek, and Roman, she handed Derek the #18. "Here you go. Once you get the food, let's eat in your convertible. It's way too crazy in here."

"Sure, babe. Way to rush the line." He pantomimed a defensive forward charging toward the quarterback. Jessica made a kissy face at him and then linked her arm through Brittany's. "Let's let the boys handle the rabid crowd."

Brittany nodded. "For sure."

She and Jessica tossed their hair in unison and strode from the restaurant, their steps in perfect sync.

It was after eight before Jessica and Brittany got back to the school. Between hanging out with the guys and then going home to shower and then taking time to redo their hair and makeup and decide what perfect programming outfits were, it just took a while before they could return.

Letting themselves in the back door of the deserted wing, they stood in the long, quiet hallway and contemplated the hundred feet or so they had to go to reach the classroom.

The hallway was only dimly lit by emergency lights, which put the bare tan walls, the scuffed beige linoleum floor, and the lockers lining the hall in gloomy shadows. The lockers in this part of the school weren't used, at least not officially. Jessica knew that some kids left messages for each other in the lockers. She couldn't help but wonder what else might be hidden in them.

Because of the empty lockers and equally bare walls and floors, all sounds seemed amplified. Jessica's and Brittany's breathing sounded like it was coming from twenty girls instead of two.

"It's so, like, creepy here when no one's around," Brittany said. Her voice echoed down the hall.

"You said that last time we had to stay late," Jessica reminded her, bumping shoulders with Brittany.

"Yeah, I probably did. But it's still true."

"Yeah." Jessica turned and checked to be sure the outer door locked behind them. When it clicked into place, she nodded. "We're locked in."

"Yeah, but, like, *with who?*" Brittany asked, visibly shivering. "You know it wouldn't be hard for some perv to sneak into the school during the day and then hide and wait until after everyone else has gone and—"

Jessica smacked Brittany's arm. "Stop it! You're going to freak me out, too." She rubbed her arms, which were now covered with prickly hairs.

"Sorry."

Jessica took Brittany's wrist. "Come on."

"We should've brought the guys," Brittany said.

"Then we wouldn't get anything done," Jessica pointed out.

"True."

"Let's go. Once we're in the classroom, we'll barricade the door like we did last time, if it'll make you feel better."

"Me? You've got goose bumps, too," Brittany accused.

"Okay, so I don't like it in here, either."

Brittany tugged on Jessica's arm. "Let's hurry."

Their footsteps echoing around them, Jessica and Brittany hurried down the hall. Neither commented when they both occasionally checked over their shoulders.

Jessica was relieved when they reached the robotics classroom and shoved the door open. Brittany scrabbled for the light switch before the door could swing shut.

The previous time they'd been in after-hours, they discovered that the classroom door didn't lock. Some discussion had ensued about whether to get over their paranoia or just give in to it. The conversation had resulted in a "give in to it" strategy: shoving one of the classroom tables in front of the door. This time, they didn't waste time with discussion. Without speaking, they moved together to the nearest table and shoved it over to block the door.

Then they both turned, exhaled, and surveyed the room.

The overhead fluorescent lights in the classroom did relieve some of the creep factor of being in the deserted wing. However, that relief was countered by the eerie presence of all the robotic parts in the room. Metal arms and heads and disembodied torsos weren't exactly comforting decor.

Jessica and Brittany went to the back of the room where Rosie still lay on her cart. Hooked up to both the wall and the laptop, it looked like she was in intensive care or something. At this point, if Rosie were to move, Jessica would have run screaming from the room.

"Um, Jessica?" Brittany said.

Jessica shook her head. "Sorry. You've got me all spooked now."

Brittany put an arm around her friend. "Come on, let's go sit and try out our new lip gloss. That will make us feel better."

Jessica nodded.

On their way over to the school, they'd stopped at the store to get some munchies in case they were here a while. Their favorite celeb had just released a new lip gloss that caught their eye; of course, they had to buy some. Brittany pulled Jessica down into a chair next to the one she settled on.

The girls applied their gloss—pink for Brittany, red for Jessica—and looked at each other. "Gorgeous," Jessica said.

Brittany grinned. "I know, right?"

Jessica took a deep breath and reached for her computer, which was just where she'd left it. "Okay," she said. "Let's see if we're good to go." She tapped a key to take the computer out of sleep mode and looked at the screen. According to the display, the upload was complete.

Jessica began tapping at keys.

"Do you, like, know what you're doing?" Brittany asked.

Jessica laughed. "Probably not. But how hard can it be?" She gestured at the screen. "See? Rosie's system is run by a software program that can be modified." She frowned at the screen for a few minutes, reading the lines of code that were already there.

Brittany leaned in and read over Jessica's shoulder. "It looks like you just input the descriptive phrases . . . like that one." She pointed to line 41 of the code, then read what came after the line number. "'Reaches out #7V800.' I think it assigns a number to the plain word commands."

"I think you're right," Jessica said, twirling a lock of super-soft hair around her index finger. "We just need to make a list of all the commands we want to program into Rosie, and then we can assign the right numbers to them and input them."

"Exactly, right?" Brittany said.

Jessica peered at the code. "Okay, realistically, we're probably limited in what we can have Rosie do, but how about we make a wish list, then see what we can do?"

Brittany nodded. "Great idea."

Jessica minimized the software screen and opened a blank doc. "Okay, so what do we want our little servants to do for us?" She grinned.

"Well, it would be nice if we never had to go get

something for ourselves." Brittany leaned back in her chair. The chair creaked, which sent a tremor down Jessica's spine. She ignored it.

"So, basically the command would be 'fetch,'" Jessica said, laughing.

Brittany broke down, too. "Yeah. Maybe just for fun, we could do 'roll over' and 'play dead.'"

Jessica threw her head back and guffawed. "Oh my gosh, stop it! That's too good!" She typed in her document, ROLL OVER. PLAY DEAD. Jessica laughed harder. "This makes me think of Titan. If he was here, he'd be giving you five."

Brittany grinned at Jessica. "They should do that, too."

Jessica nodded enthusiastically. "They should do all of Titan's tricks."

"Spin," Brittany said. She grinned. "And bow."

Jessica chuckled and typed, GIVE FIVE. SPIN. BOW.

"Okay, seriously, though," Jessica said, "this is all good for laughs, but what could they do that would be really helpful?"

Brittany tapped her lower teeth as she pondered. "Carry our bags, polish our nails—especially our toenails—dry our hair, brush our hair, style our hair . . . But first Rosie has to, like, grab those little freaks, pick them up, and put them inside her belly."

Jessica tapped the keys on her computer but then reached for the papers Mr. Thornton had handed her earlier.

"What's up?" Brittany asked.

Jessica waved her off. "Trying to figure out how we can get Rosie to recognize and make a beeline for the two brats first thing tomorrow." After skimming through all the possible commands, she noticed a section called Vocoder System.

Apparently Rosie's vocoder system, which allowed her to interpret spoken commands, could also differentiate between the voices of adults and children. She was currently programmed to approach children and avoid adults—made sense for a kiddie animatronic, she guessed. Jessica smiled. Cindy's and Mindy's chirping kid voices hadn't dropped yet, so Rosie would be sure to zero in on them. Jessica just had to take the code one step further for Rosie to approach, then grab kids . . .

As she started typing, a noise from the front of the classroom spun her around. "What was that?"

Brittany had spun, too. She was staring wide-eyed toward Mr. Thornton's desk. "I saw something move!" Brittany hissed.

"I thought I did, too," Jessica whispered back.

Both girls stood.

Holding hands, they took a tentative step toward the front of the classroom. The second they did, something shifted on Mr. Thornton's desk.

They both jumped back.

"What *was* that?!" Brittany yelped.

Jessica shook her head and frowned. She looked around the classroom. It felt like all the robot eyes in all the robot heads were watching them.

She tugged on Brittany's hand and moved forward again. Brittany pulled free to grab a robotic arm off one of the pegboards.

"Good thinking," Jessica said.

"I know, right?" Brittany nodded several times.

They crept forward together . . . until a *click* stopped them. Jessica cocked her head, listening. She heard a fluttery sound, like a bird flapping its wings.

Brittany raised the robotic arm, readying for a fight.

Jessica shook her head, but she moved forward again, looking hard at Mr. Thornton's desk. Brittany was right at her side.

Suddenly, something shot out from behind Mr. Thornton's desk and skittered over the floor toward them. Jessica screamed.

Brittany screamed, too, but she also charged. Running forward, still screaming, she brought down the robotic arm and slammed it into the ground. The impact made a metallic crack. No, not into the ground, into . . . *something* on the ground. Brittany raised the arm and brought it down again. Another metallic crack.

"What is it?" Jessica asked.

Brittany stepped back, robotic arm still poised for action. She looked down, and she didn't wield the arm again. So, Jessica stepped up beside her.

"It looks like a rat," Brittany said.

"Yeah, if rats were made of metal."

Jessica and Brittany looked at each other. "A robotic rat?" Brittany asked.

They looked back at it. A flexible steel cable originating at the back of the robotic rat twitched. Brittany stomped on it. The cable stopped moving.

Brittany looked at Jessica, frowned, and then looked around the room. "Do you, like, think anything else is going to come to life?"

"Besides Rosie? I hope not." Jessica gazed at the robotic parts on the pegboards warily. A chill slithered through her body. She shook it off.

"Come on, let's do this so we can get out of here."

"For sure," Brittany said.

Jessica sat down at the back table again and peered at her computer screen. "Where was I?"

Brittany sat down beside Jessica, still holding tight to the robotic arm. "You were putting in the 'grab the kid' commands," Brittany said.

"Right." Jessica started typing again.

When she finished, she asked, "Okay, what else do we want them to do?"

"Well, they seem pretty brainy. I wonder if their, like, brain power could, um, interface with Rosie's AI. Could they do homework for us?"

"Hmm," Jessica said. "That would be rad, but I think it would take a programmer better than me to code that."

Brittany sighed. "Yeah. Just thought I'd throw it out there."

"I like it. Maybe it's something we can add later. We could talk one of the computer nerds into helping us."

"Oh, that's brilliant," Brittany said.

"So back to everyday commands."

"Make your smoothie?"

"Good one!" Jessica typed. "And packing your lunch." She typed some more.

"Right!" Brittany said. "What about cooking?"

Jessica screwed up her face in thought, then started typing.

Brittany leaned over and watched. "Oh, basic cooking commands. Good thinking."

"It's something we'll have to do later, but I figured we should put it on the list."

Jessica sat back. "Okay, well, I should probably start coding for Rosie to pick up the girls and put them in her belly. Then I'll do the commands for getting things and bringing them to us." She started typing.

Brittany pointed at the computer screen. "I think you got that backward. Isn't that the code for the kids, not the adults?"

Jessica looked and shook her head. "Good eye. Sorry. Blonde moment." They looked at each other and laughed.

Jessica returned to typing.

The programming was a lot harder than she thought it would be, and after an hour or so, her eyes were tired. She reached up and rubbed the back of her neck and shrugged her shoulders toward her ears.

"I'd offer to take over for a while," Brittany said, "but you know I totally suck at programming."

Jessica nodded. "It's okay."

Brittany shoved her chair back. "But I could rub your shoulders for you."

Jessica smiled. "That would be great. Thanks!"

Brittany affected a British lady's maid accent. "You're welcome, milady." She started rubbing Jessica's shoulders. Then she stopped. "We should have Rosie call us 'milady.'"

Jessica grinned. "That's a great idea!" She squinted at the screen and started typing.

Jessica worked on Rosie's code for three more hours. It was after midnight when she typed in the last of the code and sat back.

"Okay," she said, "if we did this right, these commands should have been downloading into Rosie as we created them. All we need to do now is disconnect her, unplug her from the wall, and activate her."

Unplugging her computer, Jessica looked at Rosie's control panel. "She's fully charged. I think if we activate her now, she'll be good to go in the morning. Then she can grab Cindy and Mindy when they get here for their early workshop time."

"We have to be sure we get here on time so we can see that," Brittany said. She looked at her gold watch. "We won't have much time for beauty sleep."

"We don't *need* much beauty sleep," Jessica said.

They laughed. In perfectly synchronized motion, they both got out their lip gloss and freshened up their lips, then stood up from the table.

"Go ahead and activate her," Jessica said to Brittany.

Brittany grinned and reached behind Rosie's neck. She flipped a switch. As soon as she did, the cover to Rosie's control panel closed.

With a click and a whir, Rosie blinked her eyes. Her head swiveled this way and that.

Her gaze landed on Jessica. She blinked again and turned to look at Brittany.

Another click sounded from inside Rosie, and she rose up off the cart. Once she was off the cart, she stood still, looking at Brittany.

"What's she doing?" Brittany asked.

Jessica shook her head. "Maybe she's just getting ready." She shoved her laptop back into her backpack and started to zip up the pack.

Before Jessica could close her backpack, Rosie reached out and grabbed Brittany by the shoulders.

Brittany screamed. "Ow! What's she doing?"

Jessica turned toward Rosie and her friend, and she stared in disbelief. Rosie's pink hands were full-on clamped down on Brittany's right bicep.

Brittany tried to wrench herself free of Rosie's grasp, but that just resulted in Rosie's metal fingers, padded only slightly by her pink felt, digging in deeper. They cut through Brittany's bare skin, drawing blood.

Jessica watched in horror as the blood trickled down to Brittany's elbow and dripped onto her shirt. Brittany cried out, "Jessica, do something!"

Brittany tried to reach with her free arm to

deactivate Rosie, but before she could, Rosie's hydraulic-driven strength yanked Brittany off her feet and twirled her upside down. Rosie's belly access door dropped open with a hiss, and Rosie lifted Brittany out and away from her belly so Brittany was hovering in the air, parallel to the floor. While Jessica was trying to figure out why Rosie was performing what looked like an acrobatic move—she hadn't programmed that— Rosie began shoving Brittany through the access door and into Rosie's belly.

"Stop it!" Jessica screamed at Rosie. She grabbed Brittany around the waist and tried to pull her out of the animatronic pig's grasp.

What had gone wrong? Why was Rosie putting Brittany inside her stomach cavity?

Jessica had just seconds to think of these questions before Brittany screamed again. Putting aside her confusion and disbelief, Jessica yanked harder. Brittany's screams became shriller, but otherwise Jessica's efforts had no effect.

Rosie was relentlessly stuffing Brittany into her stomach. Jessica couldn't stop it.

Brittany went into the belly cavity feetfirst, and she didn't go quietly or easily. Kicking her legs madly, Brittany shrieked at the top of her lungs as she was stuffed into Rosie's open stomach. Between shrill screams, Brittany yelled, "Turn her off! Turn her off!"

Jessica let go of Brittany's waist and tried grabbing Brittany's shoulders, but obviously Brittany wasn't thinking clearly, and she squirmed wildly. Jessica finally managed to get a grip on Brittany's upper arms, but she was no match for Rosie's strength.

So, Jessica tried to do what Brittany was now chanting: "Turn her off! Turn her off! Turn her off!"

Jessica couldn't reach Rosie's control panel. Brittany's struggling torso and Rosie's relentless grasp blocked the way.

Jessica ran around behind Rosie so she could get to the switch from the other side of the pig.

Brittany kept screaming and fighting.

"Just hang on!" Jessica shouted. "I'll turn her off."

Jessica reached for the pig's activation switch, but Rosie was significantly taller than the petite teen. Even on tiptoes, Jessica couldn't reach Rosie's neck.

Leaping to try to reach the switch, Jessica failed again. She tried twice more, and finally she stopped leaping and instead grabbed a chair.

As she dragged the chair over to position it behind Rosie's back, Jessica realized that Rosie had let go of Brittany's arms. She saw Brittany twist to try to pull herself out through the open access door. But not only did her body impede her reach—as soon as Rosie let go of Brittany's shoulders, Rosie got a grip on Brittany's head. Shoving her fingers through Brittany's tidy slicked-back hair, Rosie clamped down on Brittany's skull.

Brittany's eyes goggled. They swiveled this way and that, looking for escape. Seeing Jessica, she gave her friend a beseeching look. Brittany's face was covered in sweat. In cheerleading practice, they always joked about how cheerleaders never perspired. They glowed. Well, Brittany's face wasn't glowing. It was wet with desperate sweat.

Before Jessica could say anything to Brittany to try to reassure her, Rosie shoved Brittany's head inside the stomach cavity. Brittany tried to turn and reach for the doorway, but before she could, it slammed shut with a sucking *sshhh*.

It was sealed.

Jessica stared, her mouth hanging open. She then clamped a hand over her mouth. Her friend was trapped inside Rosie Porkchop.

"Brittany! Brit? Can you hear me?" Jessica shouted.

For just an instant, the room was silent. Jessica realized her heart was pounding so hard that it felt like the rapid-fire beats were thrumming in her ears. Then, past the pounding beat in her head, she heard Brittany's muffled wail.

"Get me out of here!"

"I'm trying!" Jessica yelled. "Just hold on."

Jessica finished positioning the chair and climbed up onto it.

Brittany kept crying out and yelling. Most of what she shouted was incomprehensible, but Jessica didn't need to understand her friend's words to get her meaning. Brittany was terrified, and she wanted out of the pig. Even a moron could figure that out, and Jessica wasn't a moron.

She wished Brittany would shut up so she could concentrate, but she understood why Brittany kept yelling. Jessica would have been yelling, too, if she was stuck inside that thing.

"I'm working on deactivating Rosie," Jessica shouted. "It would help if you could just be quiet for a few seconds. I know you're scared, but your screaming is, like, freaking me out."

A couple seconds of silence passed. Then Brittany shrieked, "Being inside here is freaking me out!"

Jessica, in spite of the situation, couldn't help but smile. Leave it to Brittany to be funny in a situation like this.

"You'll be out in a few seconds," Jessica shouted to Brittany.

Jessica concentrated on reaching Rosie's controls. Even on the chair, the control box was hard to reach, but Jessica was finally able to flip the cover open. After she got it open, though, she could tell that the buttons and levers were at an angle that hid them from her view. She would have to go by feel. Reaching, she sought the controls she knew were there.

From inside Rosie, Brittany shouted, "How much longer?" Her voice was even higher than ever. And it had a catch in it. Jessica was sure Brittany was crying.

"That's enough of that," Jessica told Rosie.

Jessica fumbled around, seeking the right button. Instead of a button, though, her fingers activated a toggle switch.

Rosie Porkchop jolted so violently that she backed into Jessica's chair and tipped it over. Jessica tumbled to the ground, turning her ankle and whacking her head on the edge of a nearby table.

"Crap!" she snapped, rubbing her head.

Then she turned to look at Rosie.

She blinked in confusion.

Rosie was convulsing.

And from inside Rosie, Brittany let out a sound that Jessica had never heard before and never wanted to hear again. It sounded like a cross between a howl and a screech. It was loud—it didn't sound muffled at all— and it quite clearly was the sound of excruciating pain. The only other time Jessica had heard a sound like that was when her neighbor's cat had been run over by a lawn mower.

Before Jessica could even react to her friend's cries, they stopped.

Rosie was perfectly still.

"Oh my God!" Jessica shouted, struggling to her feet. "Brittany! Can you hear me?"

Jessica started to pant in total panic. What had happened to Brittany?

Rosie went still.

Jessica repositioned the chair so she could get a better look at Rosie's control panel. What switch had she flipped?

Jessica peered at the controls. Oh. She'd flipped the MODE switch from SUIT to ANIMATRONIC.

"Sorry," she muttered. She quickly flipped the switch back to SUIT.

As soon as the switch was moved, Rosie's belly access door popped open.

"Yes!" Jessica punched the air.

She rushed around to help her friend out of the animatronic pig.

When she stepped to the belly side of the pig, the first thing Jessica noticed was that the interior of the access door wasn't the silver gray it had been when she'd last seen it. It also wasn't dry. It was—

Is that blood?

As Jessica watched, a thick red drop detached from the edge of the door and plopped onto the gray rubber flooring. She gaped at it. The hairs on the back of her neck stood up.

Her brain was suddenly sluggish. She was having trouble processing what the blood meant. The blood and the fact that Brittany wasn't clambering to get out of the pig was telling her something. Something she didn't want to know.

Jessica blinked, then leaned toward the door, ready to help Brittany get out. "Brittany?"

Jessica tried to see inside Rosie, but she couldn't. She could, however, see a scrap of denim stuck on a gear near the door cover. A bloody scrap.

Jessica cried out and stood, shoving back the chair as she did.

In the minutes that followed, she'd have a few cogent

seconds in which she wondered if her sudden movement was what reactivated Rosie. Would Rosie have
remained dormant if Jessica had just sat there silently
until help came? Would Rosie have stayed frozen if
Jessica had slunk off the chair and retreated slowly,
stealthily, out of the classroom?

She'd never know. Because that's not what she did.
She made a loud noise, and she moved suddenly.

Rosie's reaction was instantaneous. She reached out,
and she grabbed Jessica by the shoulders.

In an identical move to the one she used on Brittany,
Rosie flipped Jessica upside down and then lifted her
into a position parallel to the floor.

Jessica screamed and started flailing around. She
pounded on the pig's hands. "Let me go!" Jessica shrieked.
Then she just started crying out for help. "Help me!"
she screamed at the top of her lungs, even though she
knew she was alone.

When she realized how futile that was, she bellowed
at Rosie, "Stop it!" This was just as ineffective.

As Jessica fought against Rosie, part of her mind—
the part that was still capable of logical thought—tried
to figure out what she had done to make the pig grab
Brittany and now her. How had she gotten the programming so wrong?

As soon as she asked the question, the answer arrived
on a fleeting second of lucidity. She'd been typing in
the name codes when they'd seen the robotic rat. Right
in the middle of that process, Jessica had left what she

was doing. When she'd gotten back to the computer, she must have flipped the codes. She'd gotten the commands reversed. Whatever she'd programmed Rosie to do to Cindy and Mindy, Rosie would do to Jessica and Brittany. And Jessica and Brittany would be forced to serve Cindy and Mindy.

Why hadn't she double-checked her work? Brittany had suggested proofreading, but Jessica hadn't listened to her. Jessica had been lazy, and given that scrap of bloody denim and the complete lack of sound from Brittany, she was pretty sure her laziness had gotten her friend killed.

Was the same thing going to happen to Jessica?

She resumed fighting the pig for all she was worth. And still, she wasn't strong enough to break out of Rosie's grasp.

But she had to keep trying.

Jessica started screaming, shrieking, wailing, howling, kicking, and punching. Whatever remnants of poise and grace Jessica used to have unraveled with every caterwaul and every primal motion she made. Jessica's presence was a thing of the past.

But none of that mattered. In spite of all her resistance, Jessica could feel her body slipping inside Rosie's. The rough edges of the belly access door scraped her hips and then her chest before rasping against her writhing shoulders.

This could not be happening.

As Jessica was crammed into Rosie's belly, she tried to grab onto Rosie's interior, hoping it would stop her forward progress. When she did, though, her hand slipped off slimy wetness. Jessica gagged and scrabbled for something to grasp, something that would help her disengage from Rosie's determined clench. But her hands couldn't find anything to help her. They just found more squishy warmth, all that now remained of her friend.

Jessica stopped using her hands to find a way to get free. Instead, she tried to look out through the opening in Rosie's belly. All she could see, because she was faceup, was Rosie's arms and the fiberglass squares of the classroom's ceiling. The bright fluorescent lights shined in her eyes, and she closed them. She opened her mouth and screamed again.

Maybe a custodian was still around, working late. Not likely. But possible. If there was a chance anyone was close by, Jessica had to keep screaming.

So she did.

No one came to help.

Just as Rosie had done with Brittany, she now clamped her hand onto the crown of Jessica's head. She steadily shoved Jessica's head inside the open belly.

Jessica noticed that the brightness against her eyelids was disappearing. She opened her eyes just in time to see that her head was passing through the opening of Rosie's belly. Just a couple more inches, and her head would be entirely inside.

Jessica gulped in air and shrieked louder than she ever had in her life. It didn't do any good.

Rosie gave Jessica one final shove, and Jessica felt the top of her head rubbing on the access door opening. She turned her head to try to see out through the opening, and that's when she saw—

Jessica shrieked again and retched. She closed her eyes tight, trying not to let her brain replay what she'd seen.

Brittany wasn't even remotely Brittany anymore. She was . . . just a churned-up mass of skin, locks of blonde hair, bits of bone, nauseatingly gleaming white tissue, and chunks of minced organs. It looked like Brittany had been pulverized and smeared all over the inside of Rosie's belly. What was left of Brittany was entangled in Rosie's mechanisms—the gears and prongs and rods— that were now drawn back against the walls of Rosie's stomach.

Jessica forced herself to open her eyes, and as soon as she did, she thought she could see jagged shards that her brain told her were pieces of Brittany's bones. She refused to listen to her brain. She couldn't. If she let herself actually acknowledge that she was being crammed into a lethal chamber that had already chewed up her friend, she would lose what was left of her mind. She had to stay focused if she was going to figure out a way to get free.

Jessica swallowed down bile, gritted her teeth, and started feeling around the interior of Rosie's belly. There had to be some mechanism that would free her.

No matter how much she searched, though, Jessica's

groping fingers found little besides gross, stomach-churning wet sponginess. At one point, she closed her fist around what she knew, instantaneously, was a piece of Brittany's intestines. As soon as the pulpy mass collapsed in her fingers, Rosie's interior was filled with an abominable smell—worse than any nastiness some skank might've left in a public toilet. Jessica's stomach flipped over in a dry heave. She opened her hand, shifted it, and tried again. This time, she got ahold of one of the sharp rods that were part of Rosie's hydraulic system. She felt blood trickle from her knuckle and wind its way down the back of her hand.

Was that her own blood? Was it Brittany's? Did it matter?

Thinking she might find something if she shifted her body, Jessica rotated to her left. Immediately, her continued shrieks crescendoed into high-decibel, glass-breaking frequencies.

Plastered to the other side of the animatronic's stomach was Brittany's face, looking like it had been peeled from her head and hung on one of the prongs that was now retracted against the inner wall. Still retaining its form, and with its bright blue eyes still in their sockets, Brittany's face was a grisly mask.

The mask was bloody at the edges, but otherwise, it looked unscathed by the destruction Rosie's systems had wreaked on Brittany's body. Brittany's irises were where they should've been. Her nose held its proper shape. And her new lip gloss, bizarrely, was still in place.

Jessica gaped at the face, unable to look away . . . until the belly access door slammed shut with a very final, very loud *WHOOSH* and reverberating *CLANK*. Then all she could see was darkness.

Jessica's shriek caught in her throat, and she started to choke. Or was that something else in her throat?

Oh God, it was. Something had dripped off Rosie's mechanisms and fallen down inside Jessica's mouth. It tasted like . . .

Jessica threw her head back and forth and spit as hard as she could. She'd tasted something coppery and salty. Jessica spit some more and tried to move her hand up to wipe out her mouth. At first, her hand got stuck between her chest and a gear. But she got it loose and wiped her palm on her tongue. She felt her stomach roil.

She was pretty sure she'd just swallowed a piece of Brittany's skin. She remembered how sweaty Brittany had looked when she'd disappeared into Rosie's belly. If her face had been perspiring, the rest of her had been, too. Jessica thought she'd just tasted blood and sweat.

"Jessica?"

Jessica froze. "Hello? Is someone out there? I'm inside here. Inside the pig! Get me out of here!"

She tried to pound on the insides of Rosie's belly, but she again encountered gears and rods. And she also, yet again, felt way too many of Brittany's squidgy body parts. She stilled her hands and listened.

"Help me, Jessica," the voice said.

Help her? What stupid girl wanted Jessica's help? It was Jessica who needed the help! Jessica opened her mouth to yell at whoever was talking. But then she stopped.

Wait a second, she thought. *That voice.*

It hadn't come from outside Rosie.

It had come from . . .

"Jessica, I think we might have screwed up," the voice said.

Jessica's breathing caught.

It was Brittany. That was Brittany's voice.

She wasn't dead?

How was that possible?

"Brit?" Jessica whispered.

"Jessica," Brittany answered. "I'm glad you're here. I'm cold."

She wasn't dead?

How was she not dead?

Jessica hadn't taken an inventory of Brittany's parts. She'd tried not to look at the gut-churning gruesomeness very much at all. But she was pretty sure she'd seen nothing but small annihilated pieces of human flesh, bone, and tissue inside the animatronic pig—that and the peeled-off face. There was no way Brittany could be alive.

"No way," Jessica said out loud.

"For sure, right?" Brittany said.

Jessica shifted her hips to try to stop a rod from pressing against her foot. She made herself breathe in and out evenly through her mouth. She wasn't going to use her nose again inside this abattoir.

Okay, so if Brittany was dead, then why was she hearing Brittany's voice?

Just as Jessica had the thought, she heard a click.

She sucked in her breath. The switch.

No, not the—

In the briefest of instants, Jessica went from thought to nothing but sensation, and the sensation was worse than any pain imaginable. Every nerve ending in her body registered a catastrophic, lethal attack, and then . . .

Nothing.

Jessica's consciousness was only darkness. No poise. No grace. No presence.

No royalty here. Nothing but blackness.

Mindy and Cindy trotted toward the door of the robotics classroom. They were a few minutes early, as they usually were. They couldn't wait to show the class later today what they'd done with the dog animatronic that Mr. Thornton had assigned to them in the sophomore class. Mindy knew Mr. Thornton would let them stand up and talk about it. They were both happy to do that.

Both Mindy and Cindy wore red today. It was a total accident. Mindy had on her favorite corduroy jumper with a red-and-yellow frilly blouse. Cindy wore a new red dress her mom had bought her at the mall the night before. It had poufy sleeves, which

Cindy had shown off to Mindy when Cindy's mom picked Mindy up to drive them both to school. "Totally mag," Mindy had said.

She and Cindy weren't too up on high school slang. That might have been one of the reasons they didn't fit in. It didn't matter. They didn't care if they fit in.

Mindy pushed on the door to the robotics classroom, but it wouldn't budge. Something was wedged up against it.

"On the count of three?" Cindy asked, turning to her friend.

Mindy nodded.

"One . . . two . . . three!" The friends heaved their full weight against the door, and it skidded open. A table was in front of it, as though someone had barricaded themselves in.

But the room was, as they'd expected it to be, empty.

Well, almost empty.

When they entered the room, the first thing Mindy and Cindy saw was Rosie Porkchop. The animatronic pig stood a few feet from the door, watching them with a happy smile. The pig's curly tail whirred in a spiral.

"Hi, Rosie," Mindy said.

Rosie raised her right arm. Both girls stared at her.

Cindy tilted her head. "I think she wants you to give her a high five."

Mindy laughed and slapped the pig's hand. Rosie stood, spun in a circle, bowed, then said, "Hello, Mindy."

Mindy raised her eyebrows.

"How does she know your name?" Cindy asked.

Mindy shook her head. "I don't know." She looked around. "Do you think Mr. Thornton programmed her with all our names?" Shifting the animatronic dog that she held, she poked Cindy. "You try saying hello."

Cindy shrugged. "Hi, Rosie." She sneezed.

"Hi, Cindy. Gesundheit."

Cindy laughed.

Rosie's voice sounded familiar to Mindy. Why?

"Hey," Cindy said. "Doesn't she sound a little bit like that mean girl?" She pulled a tissue from her pocket and blew her nose.

"Which one?" Mindy asked. She and Cindy had encountered more than a few mean girls in this school.

Mindy didn't understand at all why people picked on them just for being younger. For that matter, she had no idea why a person's appearance separated them from certain social circles. People were people. Kids were kids. What was the problem?

"The one who's going to be homecoming queen," Cindy said. "Brittany?" She wiped her nose and crumpled up the tissue.

"Oh, that one. No, the queen is Jessica. The princess is Brittany."

Cindy nodded, and her red curls bobbled around her freckled cheeks.

Mindy looked at Rosie. Did Rosie sound like

Jessica? She decided to see if Rosie would say something else.

"What are you doing here, Rosie?" she asked.

"I'm here to serve you and Cindy," Rosie said in
Jessica's smooth timbre.

"Wow!" Mindy grinned. She turned to Cindy.
"You're right. It is her voice."

Cindy nodded. She stepped up in front of Rosie's
eager face. "What do you mean by 'serve' us?" Cindy
asked the animatronic pig.

Rosie did an awkward little shuffle, then bowed. "I
am your ladies-in-waiting. I will treat you like queens.
I will do whatever you want me to do to help you and
make your life easy. Just tell me what you need, please."

"Ladies?" Mindy repeated. "There's just one of you."

"I am your ladies-in-waiting," Rosie repeated.

"Whoever programmed her needs a lesson in gram-
mar," Cindy said.

Mindy laughed. "Queens, huh?" She giggled.

Rosie nodded. "Yes, you are queens. You deserve
the best."

"I can't argue with that," Mindy said. "Can you,
Cindy?"

Cindy shook her head. She held out her backpack.
"Can you carry this for me?"

Rosie nodded happily and took the backpack from
Cindy's outstretched hands. She turned toward Mindy.
"Milady? May I have yours, too?"

Mindy snorted. "Milady? That's hilarious." She

gazed at Rosie. Rosie smiled her fixed smile back at her, waiting patiently.

Mindy shrugged. "Okay. This is getting kind of heavy." She handed the animatronic dog to Rosie. Rosie took it easily.

"I can handle my own backpack," Mindy said.

"As you wish it to be," Rosie said.

Cindy laughed and did a little happy dance. "This is the coolest thing ever!" She sneezed again.

"Gesundheit," Rosie said again.

Cindy grinned. "I love that!" She took out another tissue and honked into it.

As she wiped her nose, Cindy looked down. She frowned at the ground. "Is that—?"

She pointed at the floor, and Mindy followed the direction of her finger. She saw a drop of something thick and red. "Must be paint," Mindy said.

Mindy grabbed her friend's free hand. Together, they skipped to the front of the robotics classroom, with Rosie trotting along at their heels.

Mr. Thornton strode into the classroom as Mindy and Cindy took their seats and Rosie Porkchop set Cindy's backpack and the girls' animatronic on the table in front of them and sat down.

Mr. Thornton paused and raised an eyebrow at the pig. He looked from the pig to Mindy and Cindy and then back to the pig. "Did you and the other team, um, Jessica and Brittany, trade projects for some . . . ?"

Mindy and Cindy exchanged a glance. "Yes," Mindy said quickly. "I hope you don't mind."

Mr. Thornton shrugged. "I can't argue with the results you got with . . ." He nodded. "Well done, girls," he said. "You've tamed the monster, but let me check something . . ." He knelt next to Rosie's neck and flipped a switch. Nothing happened. He reached under her belly, felt around, then gave a tug. Nothing happened.

He straightened. "Good. Apparently, it's been deactivated."

"What has?" Mindy asked.

Mr. Thornton waved a hand as if the topic was not important. "Oh, I saw an article last night about the old springlock suits, part animatronic and part costume for . . ." He pointed at Rosie Porkchop. "This was one of them. They were taken out of commission because they were deemed too dangerous for use by . . . Apparently, sometimes these old animatronics switched modes automatically because of a glitch in the pro- gramming, so . . ." He patted Rosie's big pink head. "But she seems safe enough now, and clearly you've done a great job reprogramming her."

Mindy and Cindy exchanged looks, then smiled at Mr. Thornton. Mindy grinned when Rosie reached an extension of her front foot into Mindy's backpack and pulled out her notepad.

"Thanks, Rosie," Mindy chirred.

Inside Rosie, fused with the interlocking metal structure of the machine's mechanisms, two lifeless disembodied faces stared at each other. Although the lips on both faces had perfectly applied, shiny lip gloss, the mouths guarded by that gloss would never speak again. The two faces would stare at each other in perpetual silence, their features locked in contorted expressions of horrified understanding.

ABOUT THE AUTHORS

Scott Cawthon is the author of the bestselling video game series *Five Nights at Freddy's*, and while he is a game designer by trade, he is first and foremost a storyteller at heart. He is a graduate of The Art Institute of Houston and lives in Texas with his family.

Andrea Rains Waggener is an author, novelist, ghostwriter, essayist, short story writer, screenwriter, copywriter, editor, poet, and a proud member of Kevin Anderson & Associates' team of writers. In a past she prefers not to remember much, she was a claims adjuster, JCPenney's catalog order-taker (before computers!), appellate court clerk, legal writing instructor, and lawyer. Writing in genres that vary from her chick-lit novel, *Alternate Beauty*, to her dog how-to book, *Dog Parenting*, to her self-help book, *Healthy, Wealthy, & Wise*, to ghostwritten memoirs to ghostwritten YA, horror, mystery, and mainstream fiction projects, Andrea still manages to find time to watch the rain and obsess over her dog and her knitting, art, and music projects. She lives with her husband and said dog on the Washington Coast, and if she isn't at home creating something, she can be found walking on the beach.

Larson leaned over his desk, frowning at his computer screen. He hated following paper trails, or more accurately, *electronic* trails. All the forms, being trapped behind his desk for days at a time—it was his least favorite part of police work. He preferred being out in the field, talking to witnesses and chasing down suspects. But for all his annoyance, this kind of investigating was important, too.

For days now, he'd been trying to trace the history of the building where he'd found the ball pit. But he'd landed in a quagmire of real estate transactions and business permits. The building had been the home of so many failed ventures that trying to follow the transfers was making Larson's eyes burn. This wasn't his forte.

Larson sat back and rubbed his itchy eyes. The addresses and phone numbers were <u>all</u> blurring together.

Opening his eyes, his gaze landed on Chancey, who was strolling toward the coffee machine. Larson wasn't crazy about Chancey, but Chancey was the only other detective in the bullpen right now. Roberts and Powell were both testifying in court this afternoon, and the other detectives were out for a coffee break. At least the absence of Roberts and Powell meant the bullpen smelled better than usual. The only odor Larson noticed came from the bitter dregs in the coffee maker.

"Hey, Chancey," Larson called out.

Chancey turned, grinned, and sauntered back toward Larson. "What's up?" he asked.

Larson waved him over. He pointed at his computer screen. "You any good at tracing ownership of real estate? I've found a trail so convoluted I can't make heads nor tails of it."

Chancey pulled up a chair next to Larson's desk. The chair legs scraped across the floor. Larson got a whiff of spicy cologne.

"Sure thing," Chancey said. "That's as easy as apple pie."

Larson raised an eyebrow. "Um, okay." He pointed at his screen again. "What do you make of this?"

Chancey scanned the screen, then reached for Larson's keyboard. "Mind?"

Larson waved his okay.

Chancey took over the keyboard and typed at a blazing-fast speed for several minutes. More addresses and phone numbers flashed across the screen. Larson felt a headache coming on.

Finally, Chancey leaned back. He shook his head. "This place has had more names and owners than a stray dog has fleas."

Larson frowned. "But who owns it now?"

Chancey gestured at the screen. "Well, that there's where we get thrown off the bull. I can't figure that out from just a quick dive."

Larson studied Chancey. The cowboy persona was

annoying, but the man wasn't stupid. "Think you could if you spent some time on it?"

"I'd sure give it my best shot," Chancey said.

Larson handed Chancey part of the ball pit file. He kept back the lab results and added those to a stack of files he'd pulled a couple of hours before. "Go for it," Larson said.

Chancey took the file and grinned. Then he moseyed away to get the coffee he'd been after in the first place.

Larson looked around to make sure no one had come into the bullpen to see what he was working on. He was still alone.

Taking out a yellow legal pad, he opened the lab report and the top file in the stack he'd created, then got to work.

It took Larson an hour to finish his lists. By this time, a couple of the detectives were back, but they weren't paying Larson any attention.

Larson put down his pen and studied the pages in front of him.

Earlier that morning, he had started cross-checking the dates associated with the blood samples against dates of other crimes. He was hoping to link the blood samples to unsolved murders. That didn't happen, but he had linked them to something.

It turned out that the blood sample dates coincided with bizarre incidents, ranging from missing persons to almost every other kind of strange phenomena imaginable. In more than one incident, parents reported that their teens had found a strange, robot-like body, like a metal mannequin, not long before the teens disappeared. Larson skimmed all those statements. At first, he was tempted—like the detectives who had taken the statements—to dismiss the reports as the confused ramblings of freaked-out parents. But the details the parents gave were too similar: The body looked female, with a pale, gaunt face decorated with crude clown makeup.

Now that Larson had made his lists, he could see that a teenager had gone missing during several of the time periods associated with the blood samples Larson had taken. Not every teen was associated with the metal mannequin, but every teen's disappearance did happen on a date listed on the ball pit blood sample list. What did that mean?

The blood couldn't belong to the teens because it was the same blood each time. Who did it belong to?

Larson pushed aside his lists and started flipping through the files again. He went through photo after photo of happy or sullen-faced teens. They didn't reveal anything that he . . .

Wait a second.

Larson went back to a photo he'd just turned over. He dug in his drawer for a magnifying glass. Holding the glass over the photo, he looked past the shoulder of one of the missing girls. And there it was behind her . . . the metal mannequin with the clown face! It was real.

And now Larson knew what it looked like.

Larson examined the metal mannequin carefully. Its face was skeletal, as though the thinnest layer of diseased gray skin had been stretched over its skull. The skin was painted garishly, with a candy-apple-red mouth and pink circles on the cheeks, giving it the hideous clown-like appearance some of the parents had mentioned. Its large, deep-set eyes were dark pits, and its red-painted mouth was stretched wide, revealing a mouthful of large, jagged teeth. Larson couldn't tell if it was smiling or baring its teeth in aggression. The thing's sparse red hair was pulled into twin pigtails on top of its head, a bizarrely childish hairstyle for something so hideous. The whole thing gave Larson the creeps. So did the weird cartoonish heart pendant hanging around its neck. He wasn't sure why the heart gave him the heebie-jeebies, but it did.

Larson quickly went back through the files again, noticing something he'd missed before. He flipped back and forth through the reports. Finally, he picked up his pen and jotted a note on the bottom of his lists.

Now he had something else, too. A name.

Although most of the incidents were seemingly unrelated from a glance, someone must have investigated their connection at one point because an expert of some sort had been called in on more than one occasion, a Dr. Talbert. He apparently specialized in a mysterious material called Remnant.

Remnant, according to the investigators who'd seen it, looked like "bubbling liquid mercury," but no one knew what it did. No one had been able to get their hands on a sample of it, so it had never been analyzed.

How did all this fit together? And what did it have to do with the Stitchwraith?

Larson didn't know. The ball pit might have been visiting him in his visions, but it didn't seem to be leading him to any answers . . . at least not any answers that made sense.

Larson's only choice was to locate the Stitchwraith. The Stitchwraith was at the heart of everything. Maybe Larson would get his answers when he found it.

It had taken Jake several days, but he'd finally done it. Or at least he thought so. He was pretty sure he'd found Renelle's father.

While he nursed Renelle back to health, Jake had coaxed as much detail from her as he could about her father and where she'd lived. It had been tricky because he didn't want her to know what he was doing. He was pretty sure she'd resist any idea of going home. She clearly missed her dad, but she tensed up every time Jake mentioned him.

Jake had tried to get the information by touching Renelle, hoping to see her memories like he had seen those of the man behind the Dumpster. Unfortunately—probably because of her history with drugs—Renelle's memories were disjointed and unclear. They seemed as off-base to him as Renelle's name still felt. He continued to sense that Renelle had another name, but he hadn't asked her about it. All in all, nothing that Jake had gotten from Renelle had given him any clues about where her dad lived.

And because Renelle's memories were jumbled, Jake hadn't been able to use them to soothe her. He hadn't been able to pick a nice one and make a bubble from it like he had for the homeless man.

Even so, Renelle was much better. The food Jake had managed to get for her had worked magic.

"You're quiet tonight," Renelle said.

It was late evening. The sun had been down for just an hour or so. The night outside the shed's window was clear. A nearly full moon cast a gleaming beam of pale yellow light into the shed.

Renelle had just finished a can of fruit cocktail and was braiding her hair into pigtails. Even though she hadn't been able to wash it, it still looked pretty to Jake.

"I have something to tell you," Jake said. "But I'm not sure if you're going to be happy with me."

Renelle laughed. "You've been nicer to me than anyone else since my mom died. Why wouldn't I be happy with you?"

Jake decided it was time.

"I want to take you home," he said. He braced himself for her reaction.

Renelle tilted her head and studied Jake. Her expression didn't change. She just shrugged and said, "Okay."

Well, that was easier than he'd thought it would be. "Oh," Jake said.

Renelle laughed again but blinked as if holding back tears. "When?"

For a second, Jake was flustered. But then he stood. "How about now?"

Renelle nodded, stood, and took his metal hand. Jake pushed the door open, and together they left the shed and headed toward the railroad tracks. Renelle's home was on the outskirts of town, and the tracks led to the street her dad lived on.

It didn't take Jake and Renelle long to walk from the shed to the right street. Renelle had more strength in her legs than Jake expected.

They were walking through an area that was more rural than urban. Its houses were mostly single story and sprawling. Jake thought the style of homes here was called contemporary. He decided it wasn't something he liked. Somehow the homes didn't look very inviting. They weren't cozy and warm like the small house he'd grown up in.

When they first left the tracks, Renelle had followed Jake as if she didn't know where they were going, but now Renelle's steps were growing surer. Jake wondered why he'd worked so hard to figure out where her dad was. He should have just asked Renelle where she lived. She seemed to have no resistance to returning home . . . at least not until they reached the house.

Renelle's dad lived in a white house that looked like a collection of child's building blocks. It was even more harsh looking than the other modern houses in the area. The various chunks of the house had big windows, all covered with shades. Light filtered through the shades, illuminating a mostly concrete-and-rock front yard. *Uninviting*, Jake thought.

When Renelle's footsteps faltered on the home's front porch, Jake took her hand. "It's okay. I'll make sure he's not mean to you."

Renelle looked up at Jake. She smiled.

He rang the doorbell.

As soon as the doorbell chimed, the front door unlatched and swung open. *Well, that was weird*, Jake thought.

"Put it in the foyer," a deep male voice called out. "I'll be right there."

Jake looked at Renelle. She seemed to have gotten her nerve back. She stepped into the house as she said, "Dad must get a lot of deliveries."

Jake followed Renelle through the door, and he stopped as soon as he was inside.

The house was more welcoming on the inside. The sofa in the living room was a soothing, soft green and piled with comfortable-looking throw pillows. The coffee table was stacked with magazines, and there was a cozy armchair with a floor lamp next to it. It looked like an excellent place to curl up and read.

While Jake looked around, Renelle walked through the room as though it were an art gallery. She seemed happy to be home.

Jake gazed past her and saw a wall of photographs. He took a step toward it.

The first photo he spotted was one of two men, both wearing lab coats. One had a long, craggy face and graying bushy black hair. The other had a round face and short gray hair. Jake knew the second man. He had put together the endoskeleton that Jake was in! In the weeks since Jake had found himself in this metal body, he'd discovered that man's name was

Phineas Taggart. Renelle's dad was Taggart's friend?

Jake continued to examine the photos on the wall. Then he spied something that would have made his stomach churn, if he had had one . . . In one of the photos, Dr. Talbert was smiling happily with a preteen girl. The girl had curly black hair and dark brown eyes. She looked just like Dr. Talbert . . . *her dad*.

But wait, Jake thought, looking back and forth between the photo and the girl standing in front of it. *Renelle doesn't have curly black hair or dark brown eyes. She doesn't look anything at all like the girl in the picture.*

Larson parked on the street in front of the strange, blocky house. Chancey the Cornpone Cowboy might be annoying, but he was amazing at research. Larson walked across the concrete front yard—he guessed it saved time on mowing—and found the front door standing open.

It seemed like an invitation.

He stepped into the foyer and stood frozen, unable to believe what was in front of him. There was the familiar white face with sunken black eyes, the endoskeleton body. The Stitchwraith. Standing next to it was a young girl with unwashed hair braided into pigtails. Her clothes were worn and dirty, but she was otherwise seemed normal.

But what happened next was anything but normal.

The girl was staring at a photo of a younger girl, a preteen with curly black hair. And then suddenly, she *was* that girl—small, black-haired, adorable, and innocent looking.

Innocent looking, but not innocent.

Larson felt his insides turn to jelly. It was happening. Another one of his visions. He felt himself sinking into it, quicksand-like. He was unable to lift himself out no matter how badly he wanted to. As he stared at the newly transformed girl, the mask she had created for herself fell away. He no longer saw the smiling face of a curly-haired child but another face that was all too familiar. The sickly skull-like shape. The painted pink-circle cheeks. The red mouth with its twisted teeth. The heart-shaped pendant, which appeared to pulse and throb. It was *her* from the picture, the clown peeking over the disappeared girl's shoulder. Out of nowhere, a name popped into his head: *Eleanor.*

He could see her, but he could see *into* her, too, and what he saw was a black, chaotic force that fed on human suffering. The fear, the pain, the death—she, not the Stitchwraith, was the cause of it. In both his head and his heart, Larson knew this to be true. He was surer of it than he had been of anything in his life.

He was so sure that he drew his gun and took aim.

The girl's eyes met his. She smiled.

The room fell away, as did everything familiar.

Larson's eyelids fluttered, then shut, and he fell to the floor with a thud. "Eleanor," he whispered before he lost consciousness.

It was dark, but there was an eerie glow, as if a neon sign were shining from outside a window. But there were no windows. There was nothing. A void.

Larson blinked hard, trying to adjust his eyesight.

Then he saw her just a few feet ahead of him. She was standing in front of a table. Her back was turned, but her identity was unmistakable—the red pigtails, the long neck, the curves of the robotic body.

He stepped closer.

She was working on something so intently she didn't seem to notice him behind her. He drew nearer.

The object that was taking up all her attention was a hideous plush toy. Its long ears suggested it was a rabbit, though it was certainly the least-cute stuffed bunny

Larson had ever seen. And what in the world was she doing to it? With one hand, she held its jaws open wider than seemed possible. With the other, she was shoving something into its mouth, something that made an unpleasant, squishy sound as she pressed it down.

Stepping a bit closer, Larson saw it was a tooth, one in a row of bloody human teeth that occupied the thing's lower jaw. Its eyes, Larson noticed, were wet-looking, their whites streaked with red blood vessels. *Human eyes.* It felt like they were staring at him.

The clown girl laughed, turned around to face him, then was gone.

Larson felt the floor upturn beneath him. It tilted so far that he started sliding backward. He struggled to find his balance. Once he got his footing and the floor beneath him felt level again, he looked around to see that he was in a room, though an unfamiliar one. It was a small, modest living room. An ugly handmade afghan was draped over the couch. On the coffee table was a glass about one-fourth full of milk and a saucer with cookie crumbs on it. Where was he?

He looked around, trying to orient himself. The digital clock on the stove in the kitchen announced the time as 1:35 a.m.

There was a sound, a frantic scratching like there was an animal trapped behind the closed door of the other room. A little apprehensively, Larson opened it to let out the cat or dog.

But there was no cat or dog, and the scratching continued insistently from inside the room. Larson stood in the doorway and peeked inside. The scratching was coming from outside the window. Framed in the window was the clown-like face with the circle cheeks and red grin. She was clawing at the window with her metal fingertips. In the bed a young woman sat up clutching the covers, her eyes wide with terror.

"You need to get out of here," Larson said to the woman. "You're in danger."

She didn't look in his direction, didn't seem able to see or hear him. Instead, she looked around frantically without stopping to rest her gaze on either Larson or the murderous creature in the window, muttering, "It's the doll. It's the doll."

The floor rose up again. The bedroom fell away, and Larson felt himself falling, too.

He was standing in the doorway of an operating room. Two men in surgical scrubs stood over a table on which a motionless young boy was strapped. His eyes were open wide and stayed open even after one of the surgeons tried to close them. Behind the boy's head, holding him down by the shoulders, was the smiling clown girl.

One of the surgeons turned on a small buzz saw that whirred menacingly. Somehow Larson knew that this surgery wasn't going to save the boy; instead, it was something the boy needed saving from. It was Eleanor who was putting him in danger. Larson burst into the room, prepared to save the boy if he could.

But when Larson reached the operating table, the boy wasn't there. The surgeons were gone, and on the table was a man.

Or what was left of a man.

The body appeared to have been burnt almost beyond recognition: hairless, faceless, almost skinless except for a translucent layer through which the pulsing of his organs was visible. As Larson breathed in at the shocking sight, his nose filled with the sickly smell of charred flesh: sweet, meaty, and acrid all at the same time. He retched and took a step back.

As he tried to recover, Larson became aware of a sound—a rustling? a whisper?—that seemed to be coming from the man's body. The man's lipless mouth did not move. The sound seemed to be coming from within his chest. Larson leaned down to listen right above the man's visible beating heart.

A pair of metal hands gripped Larson's shoulders, and a familiar face burst from the burned man's body cavity. The pink cheek circles were made of the man's tissue; the mouth and teeth were red with blood. The strong metal hands dragged Larson inside the burned man's body.

There was only darkness. He tried to feel what was around him but only grasped air. Then there was a whooshing sound, and he was standing at the entrance of a maze lit by black light. It was clearly some kind of kids' game. There were colorful cutouts of buildings like a school and a firehouse, but someone must've gotten rough with the game because some of the cutouts had been knocked down, and patches were on the walls to repair damage.

And there she was in the middle of the maze like a minotaur, winking and giving a jaunty little wave before she took off at a run. He chased her, but he was a man, not a machine, and he was physically and mentally exhausted. He wasn't sure how long he could keep up the chase. He made a left, then a right, then another right, trying to remember the directions in case he got lost and needed to backtrack. His eyes ached from the harshness of the black light.

Larson made another right and ran into a boy—well, the body of a boy. The boy was hanging from the wall with wooden pegs driven through his back. A puddle of blood had gathered on the floor below his sneakers.

Larson felt he might be sick again. He turned his head from the upsetting sight and saw Eleanor leaning in the doorway, smiling as if she were looking on a happy scene.

For some reason, the dead boy was smiling, too, as if he and the clown girl were sharing a private joke.

The floor flipped up like a trapdoor. Larson fell hard

and was surprised to feel grass and dirt beneath him. It was dark, and the air was cool and breezy. Outside. He was outside. But where?

He stood and tried to shake off his disorientation. He was standing a few feet away from a railroad track. A figure was visible, standing on the tracks.

He moved closer.

Wait. There were two figures.

One was the horrible monstrosity he'd been chasing in whatever alternate reality or break with reality he was experiencing. The other, held in the arms of the first, was a kid in some kind of costume. Eleanor spun him around, no doubt making him dizzy and disoriented. The kid struggled and fought, kicking his long legs—was he dressed as a bird?—but he was tangled in his costume and couldn't get himself free.

In the distance, Larson heard the whistle of a train.

He ran to the tracks. Eleanor turned her head and locked eyes with Larson. She let go of her victim, jumped up, and took off across a nearby field. The kid in the strange bird costume was still on the tracks, tangled in his weird bird suit and disoriented.

Larson pushed him off the tracks. He landed in a ditch, but at least he wasn't in the path of the train.

Larson waited while the train roared past, then started running across the field where Eleanor had headed. But soon it was apparent that it was too late. She was gone. Larson stood in the dark field unsure of where he was or when it was.

Jake looked over at the creature he could only think of as Not Renelle. Then he looked down at the body of the police officer he had once saved. The guy had just wandered into the house and passed out, hitting his head on the floor and whispering the name *Eleanor.* Too many weird things were happening all at once.

"Renelle!" cried the same booming voice that had called out when the front door had opened.

Jake turned again and watched the bushy-haired man from the photo rush toward Renelle. *Not Renelle.*

Dr. Talbert wrapped his arms around his fake daughter and squeezed her hard. Tears streamed down his lined face. "I'm so happy you're home! I thought I'd lost you forever!"

The doctor was so focused on the girl in his arms that he didn't even look at Jake. But the girl did.

Not Renelle looked directly at Jake. And she winked.

"Eleanor," Jake said.

Eleanor grinned. The grin was even more triumphant than the wink.

Jake didn't hesitate. He launched himself at Eleanor and knocked her back into a wall of shelves.

As the metal contents of the shelves cascaded down on Jake and Eleanor, Jake thought about the last time he'd seen the thing that had pretended to be Renelle.

The last time he'd seen her, she'd been freeing herself from the trash rabbit. She was the thing that had disappeared into the vent opening. He could still hear her horrible cackle in his mind.

Jake knew now that he'd been right. This thing, Eleanor—not the man named Afton—had been the thing powering the giant monster. Afton, while unimaginably evil, had been too weak at the time. Eleanor had given him his last burst of strength; but he failed, and she escaped. And now she'd tricked Jake into bringing her here for some reason. What did she want from him?

Whatever her reasons for bringing him here, they couldn't be good. Jake figured if he attacked her before she saw it coming, he might be able to stop whatever it was she was planning.

But he hadn't counted on how clever and manipulative she was.

Jake had done nothing but knock Eleanor into the shelves; however, when she screamed and tore away from him, she had a stab wound in her belly. It was bleeding heavily.

Jake knew he hadn't stabbed Eleanor. He looked down and checked to be sure some part of him hadn't done it accidentally. He looked for sharp edges, for evidence that he had done damage. Nope. He had no blood on him at all. She'd done it to herself.

And it had the effect Jake was sure she'd planned.

Dr. Talbert cried out in rage, reached into a desk drawer, and grabbed something Jake couldn't see.

That something turned out to be a gun, as Jake discovered when Dr. Talbert fired three shots at him.

Two of the shots pinged harmlessly off Jake's metal. But the third shot hit his endoskeleton's battery.

Jake crumpled to the floor, the energy sucked out of him.

As soon as Jake was down, Dr. Talbert rushed to his "daughter." "I'll be right back, Renelle," he said. He left the room and quickly reappeared pushing a rolling metal table. He picked her up effortlessly and laid her on it.

"Hang on, Renelle," he said. "I can save you. Remnant will save you."

Jake couldn't move, but he could hear and see. He wanted, with all his will, to say, "That's not your daughter." But he couldn't speak.

As soon as Dr. Talbert said, "Remnant," Eleanor smiled.

She wanted Remnant! That was why she'd tricked Jake into bringing her here.

But what was Remnant? And why did she want it?

Flashes of the memories he felt when he was near her gave him glimpses into its nature. He couldn't hear her thoughts exactly, but he could feel the words.

Power. Life. Eternal.

The doctor put a pillow under Eleanor's head and said, "Just relax. I'll be right back." He ran from the room, then returned with a rolling metal tray containing beakers of bubbling, thick silver liquid. He pulled the tray up next to the table.

While Eleanor looked at the liquid and smiled widely, Dr. Talbert took out his phone and punched in a number. "Security? I've had a break-in. Thank you. Yes, now."

Dr. Talbert glanced at Jake. He hadn't seemed to notice the unconscious man on the floor. Eleanor gazed at the bubbling liquid as if it were the most precious thing in the world. Jake couldn't move. All he could do was watch Dr. Talbert begin hooking up tubing to the containers of the liquid substance.

Dr. Talbert glanced at Jake one more time. Then he prepared an IV to transfer the liquid into the thing he thought was his daughter.

Jake tried to will himself to move, but will without physical power was useless. The detective's eyelids fluttered and he mumbled something incoherent, but he did not regain consciousness. Eleanor locked eyes with Jake. She was still smiling.

Of course she's smiling, Jake thought. *She won.*

Something was changing. Eleanor's human disguise was disintegrating. The dark, curly hair fell from her scalp but disappeared before it hit the floor. The healthy-looking pink-tinged flesh on her face melted away to reveal a thin layer of sickly gray skin. Dr. Talbert drew back in horror. Eleanor's huge, dead eyes bulged, and her red-stained mouth gaped, revealing the vicious zigzag of her teeth. She looked at Jake, her eyes pulsating, her unhinged jaw opening wide.